STORIES TO MAKE YOU PUKE YOUR PANTS

G. Arthur Brown

PLANET BIZARRO PRESS

CONTENTS

THE HAUNTED
MONSTER

The monster could not sleep. It experienced night-mares—disturbing visions brought on by the legion of evil spirits that had taken up residence in the void where a non-monster would have a soul. Other demons clung to the outer husks of the creature, waiting for any vacancies to open up. The souls of the wicked dead stalked it like camp follow-ers. And small scurrying th things that were twisted and wrong sprouted from its spoor.

It was a haunted monster.

———◆◇◆———

There was rarely a peep in Quieton, a small town with less drama than an afterschool theater club that had never staged a single skit. Quieton was the sort of peaceful Midwest village that people often wrote about when they wanted to evoke the Everytown. But it was even quieter than that. Not quite sleepy, but it certainly went to bed early. It rolled up the sidewalks at about five PM so that you couldn't get a pizza at dinnertime, no matter how hungry you were. There was one bar and one gas station that stayed open late, but only the most desperate of locals ever ventured to those places in dire need of booze or fuel or a Slim Jim.

That all changed the night Old Eli Cole staggered, drunk and singing shanties, out into the woods near his still. That's where he first saw the Quieton Monster.

"It had eyes like the inside of Satan's ass!" he would say to passersby. "Angry and crenulated and inflamed! We all know Satan's ass is prolapsed from all the buttfucking he does, king of homos and all!" Old Eli was a very eloquent drunk and a complete homophobe, probably trying to drink himself straight. "You can't imagine how many devil horns he's stuck in there, snaking them around like he's trying to loosen a Skittles deposit. He hides his candy up there, you know! Don't eat Satan's candy, or it will turn you gay!"

He scared the shit out of all the local kids when he started babbling about the Monster everywhere he went, intermittently making the sign of the cross and taking a swig from a brown paper bag.

"You don't want to see this beast! Believe me! Stay out of the woods at night. He's such an unhappy monster that he exudes an aura of distress that gets in your hair and your clothes, like the foul smoke of burning tires."

After he tried to demonstrate the look of the Monster's eyes by pulling down his pants and spreading his ass, the sheriff finally "convinced Old Eli to leave town" permanently. And everyone forgot about the Monster for a little while.

But that's when people began to report heavy poltergeist activity. Late one Wednesday evening after returning from Bingo, Mrs. Lannegan, the elderly retired schoolteacher, saw her cat levitate, then drop back to the floor. After that, the floor lamp next to the cat shot up to the ceiling, crashed against it and broke, then fell back down. Then the sofa, the lounge chair, and the end table with the candle bowl on it, all in a line, as if an invisible home wrecker made his way from one side of the room to the other. Running the whole length of her house, the supernatural force blazed a path of moderate destruction. Very little was broken, but a lot of things were overturned, knocked over, or spilled.

"It doesn't make any sense. Why me?" she squawked to the deputy who came out to take her statement. "I've never made any enemies. Why would this ghost be taking his anger out on me?"

"Well, ma'am," the deputy replied, "I don't really handle ghosts, per se, so I'll mark this down as a suspicious circumstances case, just in the event you remember that a burglar or weird, drug-addicted grandson came in here and ransacked your place. But I'll give you the number of a paranormalist—my cousin Becca. I can't vouch for her effectiveness, but she'd really appreciate a chance to come out and investigate a real haunting."

"Haunting?" Mrs. Lannegan said. "That was a tantrum, at best."

"Ghost of a dead ADHD kid?"

"Who can say?"

He scribbled Becca's number down on a pad that said "Grocery List" at the top, ripped the page off, and handed it to the old lady.

"Don't call her after nine PM. She's got some kind of sleep disorder."*

At about seven the next morning, after staying awake all night hugging her cat tightly, Mrs. Lannegan dialed the number she'd been given. Becca sounded like a really nice girl, so she told her to come over as soon as possible to survey the supernatural devastation. As an ex-English teacher, she knew devastation was an exaggeration, but she wasn't in any kind of mood for precision of language. She wanted a ghost hunter there so she wouldn't have a repeat of last night's terror.

She'd never seen any of the popular ghost hunting programs that littered the airwaves. If she had, she would have suspected that Becca would probably be way more freaked out by the possibility of supernatural activity than she was herself.

When the girl arrived just after sunset, Mrs. Lannegan was shocked to see she looked like a child—barely out of college. In the living room, where the phenomena were first observed, Becca set up her video camera, her audio recorder to catch EVP, and a very expensive and scientific thermometer machine that recorded the ambient temperature of the room. From her pocket, she pulled a Geiger counter-type device.

"This is a PKE meter. It will pick up spiritual energy," Becca said. This wasn't precisely true, but she didn't have time to explain the intricacies of ghost hunting to a layman, even one who had been a schoolteacher.

The gizmo began making a nerve-wracking, screeching sound. Its needle wagged back and forth, going haywire.

"Uh oh," Becca said.

"Does that noise mean something bad is happening, dear?"

"Definitely getting a strong reading. It's off the charts. I should call in some backup on this one."

The gizmo burped and shrieked, jumping between high and low pitched tones. It sounded like the experimental music Mrs. Lannegan's niece made after spending half a million dollars on an arts education.

A vase toppled off the mantle, shattering on the hearth. The urn full of cat cremains immediately followed suit. Becca hyperventilated bits of dead cat, dropped the meter, and shouted, "Holy shit! We gotta get out of here!"

"Don't be a baby," Mrs. Lannegan scolded. "This isn't even as bad as last night! Isn't this what you deal with all the time?"

"I've only been out on a couple of haunting calls. Usually I just see movement out of the corner of my eye in the dark. Good thing I wore my special underwear."

The room got very cold. The two women felt very sad. Becca threw her arms around Mrs. Lannegan. The older woman clucked her tongue, then began to pat the younger woman's back.

"There, there. Nothing bad is going to happen."

Then a crash. The whole room shook. Another crash. The wall splintered and split. A bulky fist pushed through, attached to a hairy arm wrapped in decaying bandages.

"I was wrong. Something bad is going to happen," the old schoolteacher said.

After that, the video camera fell over and cut out, so we can only speculate exactly how terrified the two were before being ripped into tiny little pieces. It took a team of forensic experts—many of whom were jigsaw enthusiasts—four weeks to reassemble the corpses.

Strangely, among the carnage, there was also a penis from no known source. The tabloids speculated that one of the women must have been a hermaphrodite, but DNA testing confirmed the penis did not belong to either Becca or Mrs. Lannegan.

Both the haunting and the monster were now national news, if you count The Weekly World News as news. Every cryptozoologist and paranormal investigator that didn't already have something better to do descended on Quieton like carrion birds on a dumpster behind an abortion clinic.

———◇———

The monster did not know where it was, what it was doing, why it was doing it. It was being driven forward by the lash of an internal whip, guided by voices, toward some obscure goal. It hoped that it would find some peace when it reached that goal. Get some rest. Pulling free the women's intestines and squeezing out their contents, it moaned in agony. How had it become such a wretched thing? It could not remember.

Glancing at its left arm, it saw a bloody clump of something in its tattered bandages. It pulled the thing free. Saw that it was a dick. It had no use for dicks. The voices didn't care about dicks. What were dicks for? Tossed it away.

It remembered a time—was it actually a memory?—when it was a young cub. Things were better then, maybe? This may have been a scene from a movie it saw. Do they let monsters see movies? It may have snuck into the theater, though it had no recollection.

Bloody pudding squishing beneath its bare feet, it howled as it ran back off through the hole in the wall and into the thicket beyond, to seek as much peace as the devils inside would grant.

———◇———

Someone in Quieton had seen *Jaws*, so they called a meeting in the town rec hall to figure out how to deal with the Monster, hoping that Robert Shaw would show up and solve all their problems for them. Having been deceased since 1978 and having never been an actual shark hunter in the first place, Robert Shaw did not show up—not that a shark hunter would have been much help in trapping a land monster anyway.

In Shaw's stead stood two unlikely candidates. Hans Ondercin, the most famous bear hunter in North America (which is to say no one had ever heard of him), offered his services to trap the Monster. Jack Malone, a dried-up, old priest, shuffled from retirement to offer his services as well. He was ungainly, with the tremor of a man only recently on the wagon but was also the last of the Order of St. Ganglion, whose exorcism rites were the Cadillac of exorcisms.

The mayor, a great stuffed owl of man, leaned on the podium. A tattoo of a mermaid on his forearm was exposed by his I-mean-business rolled-up sleeves. He leaned over to speak into the tiny microphone.

"Father Malone," he croaked, "you've been retired for over a decade. Do you think you're up to the task?"

"I'm not a father anymore," the old man said, voice tremulous. "But I'll tell you what I am and what I will always be. I'm a goddamn Ganglionic exorcist. The last one. That's what I am. So I'll thank you to leave the casting out of demons to me, your honor."

A murmur of approval echoed throughout the hall.

"And Mr. Ondercin," the mayor said, "are you up to the task of trapping this so-called Monster that so savagely ripped up our beloved old schoolmarm and her young lover—"

A councilman tugged on his sleeve and whispered into his ear.

"Rather, our beloved schoolmarm and Deputy Burken's cousin Becca, who was by no means the old woman's lover, I don't care what the rumors may say."

Ondercin smirked. He was six and a half feet tall. A regular Paul Bunyan, but with bears, not trees.

"I think there was a question there for me, somewhere," he said. The audience laughed amiably. "Yes, sir. I rather reckon I'm the only feller who is going to try to wrangle a beast like this. I got my rig outside. I got guns so big, you wouldn't believe. I got a huge bastard sword too. I keep it mounted at the back of my cab. Just for show, because it looks so damn cool." He burst out laughing and began to swing an imaginary sword around over his head, switching between a one and two-handed grip.

"This is not a time for levity, Mr. Ondercin," the mayor said, looking over his glasses at the bear hunter.

"Sorry, sir. I just thought ya'll might like a display before you pay my steep-bordering-on-outrageous fee."

"I don't think you'll be killing any denizens of Hades with a sword, my boy," said the old exorcist.

"And I don't think you'll be able to keep that monster at bay with your Hail Marys, father."

"I'm not a father anymore," repeated Malone.

"And I probably got kids scattered all over the States and Canada. So maybe you should call *me* father, huh?" Ondercin said with a laugh, slapping the old man on the back, nearly toppling him from the folding chair.

"Gentlemen," the mayor said, "might I suggest that the two of you join your forces and collaborate on this thing? It seems that the Monster and the hauntings go hand in hand. You might do best to, as the kids say, have each other's back, yo."

Malone looked at Ondercin. Ondercin looked at Malone. The old man sighed. The bear hunter laughed and hoisted the little geezer into the air in one of the most monumental bear hugs that that rec hall had ever seen.

"Begorra! Save it for the bears, son!" Malone said.

"Father, er, Jack... this could be the beginning of a beautiful friendship!" He squeezed Malone even tighter.

"If you keep your friends this close, I'd hate to see where you keep your enemies."

The bear hunter laughed and kissed the old priest on the cheek.

"I love this guy!" he cried. The audience applauded.

Two boys skipped stones by the edge of the pond in the park. One white boy, one black boy. The white boy wore camo shorts and a punch-stained t-shirt. The black boy wore overalls with no shirt. They laughed and cast out more smooth, flat pebbles, dancing them across the surface nearly to the other side.

The white boy opened a paper lunch bag at his feet, handed one turkey salad sandwich to the black boy, and took one for himself. The two were friends. They had been best friends all school year. Eating sandwiches together in silence, they shared a sacred moment, for they understood that the school year was coming to an end and their paths would be separated by new class assignments and other circumstances.

The Monster raged from the bushes and tore one of the boys asunder. The other ran away, feet beating against the ground like Hell itself was on his heels, tears streaming down his face for his fallen friend.

Which boy died, you ask? Only a racist would care whether it was the white boy or the black boy. Are you some kind of racist?

———◦———

After the death of the boy, the media descended in droves, descended in torrents, descended in metaphorical hot air balloons symbolizing their empty promises. Every major outlet was represented, and they immediately began to speculate that the Klan was involved, either because the boy who was killed was black or because the boy who was killed was a white boy whose best friend was black. Does it matter? Klan involvement brought out the big guns.

They sent big city detectives to help in the murder investigation of young William Sharinghousen. Detective Reeves was a short, solidly built woman, brunette, forties, strong arms like a boxer. She picked up a thin sliver of face and winced.

"Ay, that had to hurt!" she joked to Detective Simmons, a tall, thin man whose blank stare said he was good at poker but didn't enjoy it.

"So, whatya think? Cartels? Satanists?" he asked.

"I'm thinking the townsfolk might be right. Could be a monster of some kind."

"Men are the real monsters. You know that."

"Don't go gettin' all philosophical on me, Doug," she said. "We got a lotta skin to peel here."

"Shouldn't we leave that to their CSIs?"

"I think the CSIs are busy planting corn, Doug. These little burgs aren't equipped for this level of action."

"Christ," Simmons said. "I ain't seen any shit like this since Nam."

"You weren't even alive during Vietnam."

"Past life," he said, popping the top on a bottle of Tums.

"You a Buddhist now?"

"When was I not a Buddhist?"

"Hell, Doug, I guess we never talked about religion before."

"We've only been partners eighteen months. We talk about everything during the honeymoon, what the hell are we going to talk about in the golden years?" he said, then stooped down and looked at the smears of flesh. "I could be jumping the gun here, but I think his dick is missing."

"What kind of sicko peels a kid, paints the ground with his pulverized innards, and steals his dick?"

"A monster... just like you said."

———◆———

In its den, the monster felt as if it were sleeping on a bed of nails. But it wasn't even sleeping. It was in the half-sleeping, half-waking delirium that serious insomnia sufferers know well. There was a vague notion sailing on the tide of its ebbing consciousness that perhaps the men from the town would be coming for it. It could not stay in this den forever. It would need to alternate hideouts. The basement of the ruined church. The cave in the cliffs. The top of the white oak. These would become its new haunts.

It vomited a mass of fingernails, hair, bits of partially digested flesh.

The small things worked their way forth from the sputum—grinning homunculi that bit the monster for its nourishing blood before clattering off to gather kindling to help him stay warm. A voice droned to it, reverberating inside its skull. The voice was not saying anything specific, but simply troubling the monster, moving it back to action, after which it would shut up once again. For a time.

The monster stood, sputum still dripping from its mouth. It bellowed to the sky, to cover up the sound of the voice. It pressed the button on the key fob, unlocking the door to its BMW. It ducked inside, put on the seatbelt. Drove toward the hills.

———◄O►———

Just before sunset, Ondercin set up camp in the woods where Old Eli Cole had first sighted the Monster. The bear hunter wore one of those obnoxious camouflage jackets with patterns that look like real leaves and twigs and ferns and shit. Malone sat on an overturned utility bucket. Wearing a long overcoat that he was afraid to get dirty, he griped about the bugs.

"You shouldn't wear dry-clean-only clothes on a campout, Jack," Ondercin said, putting a coffee pot on the camp stove.

"All my clothes are wool. I don't believe in synthetics."

"Never heard of cotton, I take it," said the big bear hunter, dumping coffee grounds and stones into the pot.

"Cotton doesn't hold up."

"How long you need a shirt to last, father? I've had flannels last me a decade or more."

"I haven't bought new clothes since 1985," the old priest said. "Except for some new socks in the 90s, which I darn myself."

"You do that in the night, like when there's nobody there?" said Ondercin with a grin.

"Pardon?"

"Never mind," said the bear hunter with a sigh. "Coffee will be along shortly. Say, you don't mind if I have myself a brewski, do ya?"

"No, why should I mind?"

"It's just that some recovering alkies don't want to even be around a guy having a drink. Triggers and whatnot."

"Drink and be merry, Hans. You have my blessing," Malone said with a smirk.

"The blessing of an ex-priest. I like it!"

They drank together, Ondercin having cold Moosehead, Malone sipping hot, gritty coffee. They managed to stay quiet for several hours, so as not to scare off the beast with loud noises.

Eventually, discipline gave way to boredom.

"What do you reckon Hell is like, padre?"

The old man looked wistfully into the dark sky.

"I've seen it. I don't have to guess about it," he replied.

"Oh yeah? How'd you come by that glimpse of the other side?"

"In the usual fashion. I died and went there. Got revived by a paramedic. But sure as day, I saw Hell."

"Flames and smoke? Screams of sinners?"

"Dark. Cold. I was frozen there for an eternity. When my soul returned to Earth, I'd almost forgotten what it was like to feel warmth, to be able to move. I'd been frozen solid, in blackness, like a statue."

"Well," said Ondercin with a gasp. "Do you suppose that's better or worse than a lake of fire and cackling chorus of devils?"

"Depends on how much of an introvert you are, I guess."

"As you might guess, padre—Jack—I'm a bit of the extrovert myself."

"Then I'd recommend boiling in a sea of sinners if you are given an option. At least then you can bitch to someone else instead of stewing in your own inner turmoil, considering every false move you've ever made."

"Is there a St. Peter in Hell," Ondercin said, "who plays a version of *Let's Make a Deal* with ya? And ya pick a door, and whatever sort of fate lays beyond, that's what you get stuck with?"

"I don't remember any dealing. Just freezing."

"Everything froze but your mind... that's a nightmare, alright."

"Aye," Malone said. "That's a nightmare."

They nearly jumped out of their skins and into the fire when they heard the heavy footsteps approaching their camp.

The monster awoke covered in newspapers. The night was starless.

It was not in its lair, not in anything close to a lair. It looked up at the backside of some dive in town. Standing up, it skulked from the alley, greeted by the grating cries of the copulating stray cats it nearly crushed underfoot.

Its car, when it found it in an adjacent street, was locked, and it didn't know where it might have put the keys. The interior of its head oscillated like the inside of a copper pot being scrubbed with steel wool. Electrical snaps, flakes of undigested brain raining on its psyche as it attempted to locate the lost keychain.

It stood on the sidewalk next to a storefront labeled BI-CYCLES with a small apartment atop it. It rang the doorbell and held its throbbing head. A light came on, someone in a nightshirt descended the staircase cursing. The monster did not know what time it was. The person who answered the door did not know what the monster was. The situation evolved quickly into a misunderstanding. The monster was unable to make itself understood. It was a true tragedy. Our protagonist could not make use of human modes of communication and thus defaulted to more animalistic tactics. The monster's frustration was dowsed in the blood of a person who happened to live in the wrong apartment at the wrong time. Needless to point out—the monster did not find its keys that night.

At age fifteen, Ondercin had already become known as a famous huntsman. His father had trained him up right, until his untimely death in the maw of a one-eared Kodiak at the edge of the Klondike. In the true spirit of a romantic era character, Ondercin dedicated his life to finding and killing that murderous bear. And in his darker moments, he would cut the skin on his thighs with his late father's buck knife while sitting naked in the moonlight near a brook or pond. The water was important. After the cutting, he would submerge himself for a lunar ablution. He bled out only his sadness, and the natural waters of the Earth would wash that all away.

Anyway, he was fifteen and slicing into his meaty legs. Camping somewhere outside Spokane, he'd been tracking a grizzly that had gone mad for the taste of man-meat. This was an unfortunate situation that developed because this particular grizzly was semi-domesticated. Its last owner was a former circus performer and current cannibal who had no qualms about giving his leftovers to Old Isaac, as he'd called the bear.

Now Ondercin, a fatherless young man bleeding in the wilderness, voyaged to the edge of a stream to bathe away his sins, when out of the bushes Old Isaac, smelling the man-blood, charged, snarling.

Ondercin froze, never having heard a bear snarl before.

Then a huff. The bear lunged.

Ondercin fluidly launched his thigh-cutting knife at the charging behemoth. Old Isaac fell face first, pushing up sod like a crashing plane. The blade had caught the bear right between the eyes, punching through its skull like it never would have if you or I had thrown it. But Ondercin might as well be Heracles or Siegfried or Gilgamesh.

Standing unclothed and bleeding, he snarled at the dead beast and then shouted, "I snarl, not you! Fear my teeth!" And he dove down and bit into the thing, right through the fur, and champed at mouthfuls of uncooked flesh.

That night he bathed himself in the blood of the slain and not in the stream. In his mind, the ghost of his deceased father gave him a high five.

———◦———

"What the hell are you two doing out here?" Det. Reeves asked, shining a light in Ondercin's face. Simmons' Maglite made sure Malone was also blinded.

"We're monster hunting. And get that light out of my eyes!" Ondercin said.

"You scared the living shite out of us!" Malone said.

The detectives lowered their flashlights.

"Who are you two?" Simmons asked.

"We're the monster hunters the town hired," said Ondercin. He introduced himself and Malone. The detectives gave their names, looked at each other, and asked if there was any more coffee.

The four sat around the fire, drinking coffee and comparing notes.

"You two actually think the killer was a monster," said Simmons, shaking his head.

"Not just a monster," Malone said with a grim stare. "A haunted monster, possibly possessed, certainly demonically oppressed."

"Demonic oppression?" Reeves asked.

"It's when the demons cling to the person—or in this case, the monster—but don't actually *move in*, so to speak. Slightly easier to dispel than possession, but it can be just as much torment for the sufferer."

"Do you still do an exorcism on the oppressed?" Simmons said.

"A very similar abjuration rite, like the one we do on a house that's haunted."

"Just how," said Ondercin, "does one go about telling the difference between possession and oppression?"

"You need to establish who is actually in control of the body: the person or the malevolent spirit."

"But let's use an analogy," Ondercin said. "If a guy is driving a speeding car and demons are clawing at his tires, ripping at his brakes, knocking out his drivetrain, does it really matter that the guy is steering?"

"It's a good point," Malone said. "Oppression can be just as destructive, sure. But with possession, it's like the fella is locked in the trunk, and the devils have hidden the key."

"I think I get it," Simmons said. "But either way, you gotta stop that car before you can do anything about it."

"More than that," said the ex-priest emphatically. "You have to make sure the bastard who was driving doesn't get away."

The fetid, rat-sized manikins sank mouthfuls of needle-teeth into bits of the flesh the monster had ripped from its latest victim. Dozens, if not hundreds of them, scurried in and out of masses of gore, crawling onto and into the ragged bandages of the monster. They squirreled away innards for the dry spells between slayings. The severe lack of refrigeration may have accounted for the stench which trailed the thing. The monster recoiled from ghostly cries, the wails of the souls of the fallen who shadowed it for reasons it did not understand.

In some way, the monster felt, the parasitic creatures and spirits were aiding it, easing its progress toward the goal of becoming less haunted. It smiled as a frenetic imp stabbed a straw into its massive eye and sucked out a small measure of humor. The less bodily fluids inside it, the quieter the voices seemed. Sometimes the monster would allow itself to bleed, just to weaken the clout of their imperious judgments. The creatures' feeding on it was symbiotic.

One squamous imp slithered up the monster's neck and forced a bit of kidney into the monster's mouth. This was the closest to happy and lucid the monster ever got. It savored the morsel, but soon it was chewed and swallowed and out of mind.

The grief layered itself back onto the monster as the little things clambered aboard and nestled in for the journey. The journey? Journey to where? The monster did not know. A howl at the moon, and it was off again.

———◦———

Back when he was a man of no more than thirty, Father Malone stood in the antechamber, admiring the engravings of saints being boiled, burned, beheaded, beaten, and otherwise brutalized. That was the way you had to make it in the Church: a well-documented and picturesque martyrdom, virginity intact if you were unfortunate enough to be born without a penis. St. Ursicinus, complete with his book and lilies, was hanging by his stiff neck. Wearing ice skates, St. Lydwine lay impaled on her own broken rib. St. Ganglion, a look of dismay on his face, rubbed his swollen wrist.

"Those fellows and fillies really knew how it was done," Malone said with an appreciative sigh.

"You have to be pretty groovy to get an engraving on these walls," said the abbot, emerging from a conspicuously small door that he had to stoop to pass through. The man was early fifties and average height, wore a paisley habit and small, round spectacles with light purple tinted lenses. "And St. Ganglion was truly the grooviest of them all. Far out. Massaged his cyst away. Massaged his entire existence away. Massaged himself directly to Paradise to sit at the right wrist of Christ."

"He was a great man," Malone said reverently. "My order, as you well know, was founded on his example."

"I was examining *The Golden Legend* last night as I retrieved these relics for you. Ganglion was outta sight in every respect. One of his miracles was becoming invisible to escape from the clutches of that fink, the evil Emperor Crustaceus."

"While I normally wouldn't consider evasion a noble endeavor," Malone said, "Crustaceus would have eaten him had he not. He would never have been able to exorcize the beautiful orphan twins for which he is so well remembered."

The abbot unrolled a cloth on the table at the center of the antechamber.

"There," he said with awe in his voice. "There it is. The Wristband of St. Ganglion." The Wristband was little more than a bit of a filthy rag, stained by blood or worse over a millennium before. "I nearly went ape the first time I laid eyes on this beauty. A lot of hodads just can't dig the power contained herein, man."

"If I am entrusted with the Wristband, that means I'm truly the final member of the order."

"Yes. Sadly, Father Laurence, the last of your brethren, passed away last week. He was totally shot up with cursed bullets."

"How could they tell they were bewitched?"

"Vatican Forensics could make out little devilish glyphs embossed in the lead."

"Diabolical," Malone whispered in disbelief.

"You ain't kidding. So it falls to you, Father Malone. The fate of the Order is now resting heavily on your shoulders."

Malone was overwhelmed, even vexed, that so much pressure was put upon him so early in his career as an exorcist. He'd only led one rite on his own before his mentor, Father McDermott, died mysteriously of an ancient family curse. It was hardly fair to entrust the mission of an entire order to a rookie like himself. But he took the small bit of cloth in hand, and in doing so, he felt a sort of transfiguration, instantaneous, like baptism by bloody rag. A zeal filled him that he'd never known.

He turned and left the antechamber.

"Wait!" the abbot called after him. "You've forgotten the Sacred Comb!"

The words fell on ears deaf with devotion.

Two decades later, after a brush with death, Malone hung up his robes. When the Church sent an envoy with blandishments to entice his return, he turned him away. And when the envoy asked for the safe return of the holy relic known as The Wristband of St. Ganglion, Malone shrugged and said it had been lost in the chaos of the last rite he'd performed—the one that nearly killed him.

The Church was not pleased. They took Malone off the mailing list and told him not to attend any more potlucks, which was just as well by him.

———◄O►———

"What was that?" Simmons said, shining his flashlight into the trees nearby the camp.

"I heard it too," said Ondercin, grabbing his large harpoon gun as he rose from his folding chair.

"Who goes there?" Malone feebly squawked.

Something, a large something, moved quickly away. But the flashlight had caught it there not twenty yards from camp. The Monster.

Ondercin ran after it, and the two detectives quickly followed.

Malone was left nervously fiddling with his flashlight. He couldn't figure out how to turn it on. And so, looking foolishly into the bulb, he accidentally slid the switch, temporarily blinding himself.

"What the hell?" shouted Ondercin, stopping. About hundred yards from camp a dead body lay on the ground. A man, dickless, partially decomposed. The bear hunter damned himself for becoming distracted. He waved the light around, looking for any sign of where the Monster might have gone.

Simmons checked the corpse's pockets for ID. "His name is Eli Cole."

"That's the feller who first saw the beast," Ondercin said, still searching frantically for any signs of movement. He gave up and started tracking the Monster by looking for footprints. He could see none, but he did see some small things. Living things, or at least, moving things. He picked one up. It appeared necrotic and full of postmortem lividity, yet it bit his finger, causing him to drop it. It rapidly hurried away into the undergrowth.

"Christ! What was that abomination?" Malone said, having finally caught up to the others.

"I don't know. But maybe," said Ondercin, following it with the light beam, "we can follow it back to its mama."

"You mean papa, don't you?" Reeves said absently, surveying the area around Eli Cole's body.

"I don't think we quite know the sex of the Monster at this point, ma'am," Malone said.

Ondercin edged forward on the trail of the small creature. "Shit! There's more of these things. They must be some kind of parasites, like fleas, living on the Monster."

He progressed a few feet, seeing more and more of the small things. They scampered toward him, grabbing at his pants, climbing his legs. One or two sunk their tiny fangs in, breaking the skin.

"Uh oh!" he cried. "I wasn't really prepared for this."

"But I am," Malone said, pulling a small canister from his pocket and spraying the creatures. They squealed, writhed, fell to the ground, and clattered away.

"What was that? Holy water?" Reeves asked.

"Close. Bug spray," the ex-priest said coldly. "I hate bugs."

"I don't think those are bugs, padre, er, Jack," Ondercin said, still checking himself to ensure there were no stragglers.

"They are no earthly bugs, but they still respond the same," Malone said.

They all looked around. Flashlights darting here and there. No sign of the Monster.

"What now?" Reeves said.

"Shhh," Ondercin said, waving his free hand. "I think I heard something."

They all stopped talking, stayed perfectly still.

Nothing.

"I coulda swore—"

Something huge and hairy was on Malone in a flash. The old ex-priest, able to keep his wits about him, spritzed the area where he theorized its head should be with the bug spray. The thing hissed but was hardly deterred.

Ondercin, taking the huge risk of hitting the priest, shot the thing in the back with a harpoon.

The Monster roared. The roar woke up all the sleeping birds in the trees and sent them screaming into the night sky. It tossed Malone aside and fled, leaving a trail of blood.

Ondercin picked up the old man. "Are you okay, Jack?"

"Yes, I'm alright. I don't think it wanted to hurt me."

"Why would you say a nutty thing like that?" Simmons asked.

"It whispered something. Sounded like 'I just want to find my car keys.'"

"Look, Jack!" Ondercin said, shining his light on the torn arm of the ex-priest's coat. "You're bleeding." His skin was ripped as if by a talon.

"I don't think it knows its own strength. Look, I'm not saying it isn't dangerous, but I don't think it knows what it is doing."

"Well, shit, Jack," Ondercin said. "We've still got to trap it and subdue it before we can figure out what it is and if it can be helped."

"But it's gone now," said Malone.

"Trail of blood should be easy enough to follow," Simmons said. "I'll come with you, Ondercin. You can track it."

"I'm afraid," said Reeves, pistol leveled, "that none of you bozos will be doing anything of the sort."

"What in the name of Jesus?" Malone said, standing up so quickly that he lost his balance and wobbled.

"Drop your weapons, gents."

Ondercin and Simmons obliged.

"Ay, Doug, did I ever tell you I had a brother?"

"No, no, you never did. But this is something that I shoulda seen prefigured in some of our conversations leading up to this point. Kinda really feels a bit, I don't know, out of the clear blue sky."

"It's night time. The sky is black," Reeves said.

"Figure of speech."

"Yeah, maybe you and me shoulda talked more about religion, Doug. Because then maybe I woulda told you that my brother and I come from a long line of devil worshippers who were doing their damnedest to bring about Armageddon by creating an army of haunted monsters."

Malone scoffed. "Does anyone even bother to read the goddamned Bible anymore? There's no 'bringing about Armageddon.' It's the Lord's plan and it leads to the destruction of Satan and all his minions. What devil worshipper would want to bring that about?"

"You have been reading the wrong Bible, Malone," Reeves said. "We've got the original texts translated from a tongue so archaic that it was already forgotten before Methuselah was in diapers. Only the spirits of the Ancient Ones are able to read it. It was freaking torture to track those assholes down, but we managed it. So, only *we* have the truth."

"Why haunted monsters?" Ondercin said.

"Ordinary monsters and hauntings are just too played out. We needed to up the ante."

"Still feels outta nowhere," Simmons said. "I thought I knew you. This is pretty damn far out of character. It's going to take me a moment to process."

"And it's only going to take you a moment to die too," Reeves said, stepping toward him and pointing the barrel right as this forehead.

Malone muttered something under his breath.

"What are you babbling about, old man?" Reeves said, her eyes darting between the three men.

The ex-priest continued to mumble.

Ondercin gasped.

The corpse of Old Eli Cole rose, surrounded by a blurry, blue-white luminescence.

"What the fuck?" Reeves shrieked.

"I am St. Ganglion," the living corpse said. "Who dares to haunt monsters in my presence?"

"I am a Scion of the First Baal!" Reeves cried. "You have no authority over my lineage!" She ripped open her coat, then her blouse, and revealed an amulet bearing a glowing insignia.

"Raaaaaah!" St. Ganglion shrank back at the sight of the talisman. "Good heavens!"

"Surely," Malone said, "this woman's black magic is not so strong as to overpower the one and only St. Ganglion, forefather of the Order of Ganglionic Exorcism!"

"She's right, damn it all," St. Ganglion said. "I have no authority here. Shit, I've failed you, son." The corpse of Eli Cole folded upon itself. The glow dissipated.

"Well, *that's* a letdown," Ondercin said, shaking his head.

"Now perhaps you see," Malone groaned, "why I'm an *ex*-priest."

"And you're about to be an ex-liver," Reeves said, turning the gun on Malone.

"Ex-liver?" Simmons asked.

"Shit, Doug. Sounded a lot better in my head. I apologize that my murder banter is not more advanced. That's not really something my cult puts much focus on."

"Okay," Ondercin said, "lemme see if I can figure this out real quick, because I'd hate to die all confused. Your brother made the Monster?"

"No, where'd you get a crazy idea like that?"

"It's not exactly clear what all this is about," Simmons agreed.

"The Monster *is* my brother. All monsters are made out of devoted cult members. And my brother was the most devout of all."

"Remind me not to join that cult. Am I right?" Ondercin said with a nervous chuckle.

"So, I'm still not one hundred percent clear," Malone broke in. "Are you protecting the Monster because he's your brother, or is this something you do for your cult?"

"It's not one or the other, okay. I became a cop to be on the inside and help cover shit up for the cult. I also happen to love my brother, even if he is a rampaging, mindless monster. Why am I explaining this shit to dead men?"

She cocked her automatic pistol, which is something that only happens in really special b-movies.

"Domine ominus et omnibus!" cried St. Ganglion.

Reeves spun to face the reanimated corpse, but it was too late. Her gun was ripped from her grasp by the dead hands of Eli Cole. Simmons rushed her, forced her to the ground, and cuffed her hands behind her back while she panted feebly, "I can't breathe."

"St. Ganglion, you old trickster!" Malone said. "Praise the Lord!"

"Yes," said the saint, "I normally don't resort to guile in situations such as this, but I felt it was the only way to save you three, for which I will be known in future tales told by the members of the order named in my honor."

"Yeah, about that..." said Malone, but he was unable to finish his thought.

Somehow aware its sister was in danger, the Monster charged from the darkness. It tackled the reanimated drunk, tore the body to tatty bits. The luminescence died away. The Monster snarled at Ondercin.

"Oh my God," Ondercin said. "It's missing an ear! It's the Kodiak that killed my dad!"

"Are you mad? That's no bear," Malone said, running away.

Simmons opened fire on the beast but was swatted aside. He landed awkwardly, too dazed to stand.

Ondercin stared the thing down at close range. The Monster was a huge man in a bear skin, with bandages wrapped around its body, holding the pelt in place. It swarmed with moving things, and wisps of mist seethed from it, surrounding it with a phantasmal fog. And there were sinister voices if you listened closely enough. It was a haunted monster.

When he was at a safe distance, Malone began to recite the Rites of St. Ganglion as best he could remember them.

The Monster shrieked as if in response.

The great bear hunter gnashed his teeth and advanced, empty-handed, moving with the power of a charging rhino. The Monster was a head taller, but Ondercin had no problem knocking it down. He pounded on the thing's face as the Monster clawed wildly at the man's chest and belly.

Ondercin felt a chill and an overwhelming sense of desperation. Then paralysis overtook his limbs.

"Jack! Something's wrong!"

"Detritus rectue delirium!" Malone shouted.

The eerie mist stopped pouring forth from the Monster.

"Hans!" Malone cried. "I think I've given you a reprieve from the haunting part!"

"So, now he's just a... a monster?" Ondercin moved his arms, freed of the spiritual grip of the Monster's demons.

"Temporarily! It's as if I've paused the spiritual activity. Hit the spectral snooze bar, if you will."

Ondercin pounded away on the head of the beast. "How much time do I have?"

"Not long! Go for its heart!"

The hunter summoned some hidden inner strength, grabbed the Monster's flailing arms, and snapped both humeri, reducing the thing to a whining mass of dead bear skin and smelly bandages. Snarling, Ondercin tore at the chest to expose bare flesh, homunculi scurrying clear. Then Ondercin bit into the man inside the Monster. Bits of skin and connective tissue stuck in his teeth. But he summoned his totem animal, the timber wolf, and used that power to champ not only through the flesh, but through the breastbone. Ondercin surprised even himself. He sat back and spat out a mouthful of mangled muscle and bone, then plunged his fist into the chest cavity and squeezed the heart until it popped like a balloon full of Jell-O.

The Monster was dead.

Its killer breathed heavily.

Malone approached, asking, "Are you all right, lad?"

Ondercin did not respond.

Simmons sat up, holding his head.

"What the fuck just happened?"

"I think," Malone said, "we did it."

Simmons stood and wandered over to Reeves.

"Oh shit," he said. "I left her face down here, and she suffocated."

"Well, I suppose that's just as well," Malone said. "She was an admitted devil worshiper who was going to kill us all and allow a monster to roam the land and kill innocents. Also, she was trying to cause the end of the world."

"It's just," Simmons said, and paused. He wiped his brow. "It's just going to be a shitload of paperwork."

Ondercin stirred, looked at Malone. "Well, that was shitty. I really didn't expect to have to do that tonight."

Malone put his arm around the big man, still atop the corpse of the Monster.

"So," Simmons said, "that's just a guy in a bear suit with mummy bandages?"

"Let's see who he is under the mask made of the Kodiak that killed my dad," Ondercin said. He pulled the bear face free, exposing the visage of a man wearing light purple tinted spectacles.

"I-i-it can't be!" Malone sputtered. "The abbot!"

It was indeed the same abbot who had given him the Wristband that allowed him to summon St. Ganglion.

"Well, that doesn't make any goddamn sense," Malone said. "Wouldn't he be over ninety now? And he's only like five-foot-nine. The Monster was eight feet tall!"

"I guess we'll chalk all that up to black magic and whatnot," Ondercin said. He rose, wiped some blood on his pants, looked up at the moon through the canopy of trees, and said, "I really need a stream or a lake to bathe in."

"I saw St. Ganglion tonight," Malone said distantly. "In the flesh, or rather, in *some* flesh. Not his own. I've got some serious rethinking of my faith to do."

The two shuffled off aimlessly into the night.

Simmons called after them: "Hey, you can't just leave! This is a crime scene. I'm going to need statements!" He looked at his dead partner, the pulverized monster, and the slivered bits of Eli Cole.

"Fuck it. I wasn't even here. Yeah, she went out here on her own. Someone else can handle this."

He shuffled off aimlessly into the night.

I TOOK ONE APPLE TO THE GRAVE

"Are there wolves, Leonard? I can hear them panting. Please say there are wolves," the old man rasped from his bed. He stared blankly toward the ceiling, having finally succumbed to blindness some days ago. He was delirious again, and the spells were becoming more frequent.

Leonard shouldered his musket and stared out the wavy glass of the bedroom window into the cottage yard. "No, sir. No wolves today." He loosened his chinstrap, keeping his head exceptionally still to not topple his tall shako. He leaned forward for a better view, jostling the tassels of his epaulets. The substantial fog obscured his vision so that only the barest yards beyond the window were discernable. In that space, there was a veritable absence of wolves. Neither were there mountain cats, bears, boars, nor stags. There was the dead grass of midwinter, gray and brittle. There was the split-rail fence, falling down at several adjacent sections—not that the fence would have stopped the wild beasts had it been intact. Leonard, aware of the imperfections in the yard's perimeter, remained entirely unconcerned by the prospect of wolves at that time.

"I am put at ease," the old man said. He wheezed for a time and then said, "But it is also a shame. In my youth, you could not throw a stone without hitting a wolf. Farmers and hunters have killed or chased them all off. I'll be lucky to live to see another. The last time the wolves came, no one could see them. I just heard their heavy breaths. They were too cunning to howl. A secret mission. A moon mission, in the moonlight."

A knock came at the rickety bedroom door. "Captain Kaspar?" a muffled voice said.

Leonard approached the door and opened it only a few inches. "The captain took the others on patrol."

The old man's nephew, Michal, scowled at Leonard. "Why did they leave only you to guard my uncle, sergeant?" His thick, dark eye brows and prune-shaped nose contorted to make his face even uglier than Leonard usually found it. Michal was a bald hobgoblin of a man who Leonard wished would simply vanish from existence. He'd been a constant pain since the troop had arrived.

"I am perfectly capable of protecting this household. The captain had other matters to attend to."

"It's only that we had a deal, you see. Captain Kaspar was given money by me, and I was given certain assurances by him."

"No agreements have been violated. The old man is here in bed, under my watchful eye. This house is still standing. The livestock have not been killed or ravaged. The captain will return in no more than a few hours. Until then, I'm here to assist."

"All right," said Michal, turning about to descend the stairs but casting a quick eye at the ailing elder. "Just don't let him get away with anything. That old bastard is as mischievous as an imp."

"I can still hear, dear nephew," called the dry voice of the old man. "I can hear you breathe. Like you've a wolf inside your lungs. Tonguing its way up your windpipe. Gouging at your throat."

"No, sir," said Leonard, shutting the door. "No wolves here."

———◦———

There were two men in the uniforms of Austrian lieutenants. They trudged through calf-deep snow in a valley, shivering, teeth achatter.

The taller one said, "And there will be a ship, you say, to deliver us home?"

The shorter said, "That is what Kaspar told me. I did not question his directives. He's a captain."

"But we are in the middle of a frozen waste, surrounded by mountains. Where could there be a port? And what kind of ship could break the ice that no doubt keeps their harbor locked?"

"I'm telling you, Kaspar assured me. He does not give his assurances lightly."

"This I know."

"I should hope so."

"I should hope we find some blankets in the next few minutes, or it shall be a freezing death for the two of us."

"Quite."

As they broke into a larger clearing, a ray of sun shone down through a spot in the gray, oppressive cloud cover, striking the over-sized flakes of falling snow, making them shimmer with tiny crystal rainbows, which the two took to be good luck. And in the next moment, they saw a village. The houses were of snow. The barns were of snow. The pale was of snow, and the watch tower was of snow. All that stood about in that village were snowmen.

———◦———

Myska, Zaba, Jezek, and Meinrad lounged beside the hole while Vilmas continued to dig. Their uniforms were dirty, torn, and weather-beaten. They'd removed their jackets and laid them across a fence rail. The heap of loose dirt next to the large hole stood as high as Zaba, the shortest man in the group, and still, there was digging to be done. Myska whistled a funerary dirge, though the sound was more of an annoying chirp.

Jezek bristled at the shrill tones and griped, "If only it was not so wet out. The fog, it soaks me through. Two minutes of digging and my sweat makes a home in my clothing." He removed his cap and ran his dirty fingers through his dark, coarse coiffure. "Sopping hair! My cap is thoroughly sodden! It would kill Dadzbog for one day of no fog?"

Zaba's gut waggled as he guffawed. "The wet is fine. The sun brings heat, and the heat brings more sweat. You'd be no drier then, you superstitious clodpoll. It's the Age of Reason, my friend. There is no room for the stupid gods of your grand-parents."

"I expect no less than blasphemy from a sluggard like you, Zaba! May Dadzbog turn your mouth to the back of your head so that you can't see what you're eating!" Jezek said and spat thrice into the pile of earth.

Meinrad tugged at his Van Dyke. "I think what Zaba means is that the new science shows us the complexity of the world—of the universe. Simple gods worshipped by peas-ants or idols carved by the heathens of distant tribal lands could never possibly hold sway over its intricate complexi-ty. Nature moves like a well-oiled machine, all the parts in perfect alignment, with amazing synchronicity between very disparate mechanisms. The gods necessary in this age would have to be educated in cosmic universities, learning the arts and philosophy and mathematics, spending many years in the laboratory and in the field before even attempting to so much as create a potato."

"This sounds like the method of my wife," said Myska, simpering. "She spends all day doing the cooking to make me only potatoes at dinner time!"

"I have heard," croaked Zaba, "that Myska's wife practices strange mathematic figures with the other men in town while he's away in the army."

"They put into practice Greek philosophies!" chattered Jezek.

They all laughed but Myska, who hung his head and nodded. "Laugh all you like. It's hard being a cuckold, but at least my wife doesn't have a cock like Vilmas'."

Vilmas, a hulk of a man, threw down his shovel and scrabbled up the side of the pit. Jezek and Meinrad, the two added together hardly bigger than Vilmas, could barely stop him from attacking Myska, who cowered behind Zaba's girth.

"You are a brute! A simple, boorish brute!" squealed Myska.

"I'll crush you under my heel and won't think twice about it, vermin," growled Vilmas. "You blasted Bohemians are all sniveling, lickspittle worms. One day, Myska...." He backed away, and the others released their grip on him. Walking backward, he maintained eye contact for a few steps, then turned and hopped down into the hole.

"Bounder," muttered Myska, eyeing the larger man fearfully.

"Let it be," hissed Zaba. "Anyway, it's long past time to start up digging again. Vilmas can't do this alone."

"I *could* do it alone, fat guts."

"Yes, sure," Zaba said. "But it would take you all week."

"Time, I've got," groaned Vilmas, shoveling out a large rock. "But my patience runs short."

"We are never going to find the box, are we?" said Jezek, hefting his shovel onto his shoulder, then dropping down at the edge and lowering himself in.

"I hope that we find the right box," said Meinrad, driving his spade into the earthen wall of the pit.

"You are saying there could be a wrong box?" said Zaba, already panting.

"Always two boxes," said Jezek. "Everyone knows that, right? One has a live cat inside. One has a dead cat inside."

"Three hundred devils! May God let their seed be wiped out," said Myska, stopping work for a moment. "I am allergic to those pests." He spat on his blistered hand and placed it back on the haft. "Are we seriously looking for cats?"

"I know your mother has a furry little cat," said Zaba.

"May a dog be infected by *your* mother!" shrieked Myska.

"Fellows!" barked Meinrad. "We have a job to do."

"And don't open the box when you find it," Vilmas said. "I told you this already, but I'll tell you again. Like the thin one said. Always two boxes, and you wouldn't want to be he who opens the wrong one."

———◇———

"When I was a child, the wolves always came. We could hardly keep them off the flock." The sheep had died, Leonard knew, but the old man was too feverish to remember. "The wolves will be back."

"Perhaps, sir," said Leonard. "But when, I cannot say."

A soft knock came on the door.

"Who goes?" Leonard said.

"Sergeant Leonard?" a soft voice replied. "I didn't know you had stayed behind." A hunchbacked young man entered, dragging a broom. "You are wearing your cap."

"They left me to guard him. I'm on duty."

"He doesn't look very well, does he?" the hunchback said, then sucked his teeth.

Leonard listened to the sound of the old man's breathing. "He's blind, not deaf."

The hunchback knelt at his grandfather's side, resting his head on the bed. "Grandfather, can you hear me?"

The old man's brow beaded with sweat. "Who is it?"

"It's Wasilly, Grandfather."

A coughing fit racked the old man's body. Leonard winced and peered out the window.

"Wasilly. Bartos' boy, isn't it? A lad no older than seven."

"Grandfather, I am a fully grown man now. Nineteen years old."

"A cripple, too, as I recall. We were tempted at times to use you to bait the wolves."

This struck Leonard as a particularly cruel thing to say to one's kinsman, but Wasilly just laughed.

"Oh, Great Uncle," the hunchback said, "you have always had that unkind sense of humor."

"Isn't he your grandfather?" Leonard said.

"No, why would you think so?" said Wasilly.

"You've been calling him *Grandfather* the whole time."

"Why would I call him that?" The hunchback began to sweep, stirring up small dust clouds from the cracks in the floorboards. He whistled a dark, Slavic folksong that Leonard thought he recognized.

"Dark day when the maiden died," the old man sang languidly along. "I took one apple to the grave, and I returned with two apples. One apple I did give the hairy boy I met along the way. I showed him kindness by not wringing his neck. He was an abomination. Heigh-ho! Dark day when the maiden died."

"Are those the actual words?" Leonard asked.

Wasilly stopped whistling and said, "It's an old regional variation. The more common version goes like this: I was in town on the day, the day, the day, the dark day when the maiden died. I took one apple to the grave, I took, I took, I took one bite. Heigh-ho! On the dark day, the day, the day, the dark day when the maiden died. I took a boy behind the shed, I took his head, I took his head. Spilled his blood upon the grave, the lonesome grave, the lonesome grave. I took an apple from his head, I drank his blood like cider. I made his neck into a stew, I bobbed for his eyeballs. His dark eyeballs, his dark, his dark, dark eyeballs in the tub where the maiden did bathe."

Leonard found the lyrics foolish and confusing. He had never really understood the locals at all. "It's too long," he said and stared out the window at a rabbit hopping along by the fence.

"As long as it tells a story, who cares how long it is?" the old man said. "Look at the sagas of the Northmen, or the epic poetry of the ancients, or the scriptures, or the book of things not yet invented. Very long indeed, and only the last has no real story. Or should I say, has no interconnected story between each of the things not yet invented. If they are not yet invented by different men who will never meet, perhaps even never live at the same time, then there is nothing to be said. I don't know why I put that one on the list, except that it is oh-so-very long. But worth a read. Would that I could get my sight back now and the use of my legs so that I could walk to Borislav's farm, and would that I could beat him senseless with a rake and take back my treasured tome. He said I didn't deserve such a special book, which he said was only for prophets, which according to himself he was."

"I told Bratumila of that book once," Wasilly said, "and she told me I was a fool to think such things as those in the book would one day come to pass. For instance, the book tells of a bird-machine that flies men through the air and even past the sky. Her prediction is that men will only ascend the heavens in balloons filled with hot gas, or by being shot from extremely large cannons. I told her that she didn't know anything, she's only the milk maid. And she told me not to bother asking for her hand in marriage. Though, if I am being honest with myself, it could be my limp that has put her off me."

Leonard tried not to laugh at the idea that Wasilly's problem was merely a limp. The twisted man was having trouble wrangling his broom, and the room seemed no cleaner than before he had started.

"I've got blisters on my fingers!" The hunchback said, tossing aside the broom and sucking on his gnarled hand. His mouth opened like that of a bullfrog. He could fit almost the entire hand inside.

Leonard turned away, glanced out the window, and caught sight of a girl child in a bright red dress prancing through the dreary yard.

"What does the part about the apple mean?" Leonard asked.

"Eh?" Wasilly said, pulling his hand free. "Oh, in the song?"

"It means when you go to a maiden's grave," croaked the old man, "you don't go empty-handed unless you want to get haunted! What do you think it means, you foolish Austrian! Go back to your mountains and leave us in peace!"

"Calm down, Grandfather!" shouted Wasilly, pitifully.

"See! You called him Grandfather!" Leonard said.

"It's the language barrier. You don't understand the inflections of our dialect, you see? It is all about the nuance. One nuance is that I say *grandfather* in such a way that it means, literally, *grandfather*. Another nuance and *grandfather* means *great uncle*. Do you see?"

"Honestly, gentlemen, I'll be glad when this assignment is over and we leave your village. I feel quite out of place here."

"Oh, then you will be going?"

"I hope to. I wish to."

Eyeing the soldier uncertainly, Wasilly asked, "Could I hold your musket, sergeant?"

Leonard scoffed. "Why do you want it?"

"It will make it easier for you to take up the broom and finish sweeping. You see, my bone ache has returned. My blood is also very sore. I cannot finish the chores today, and today is chore day."

"I will not sweep your floors. That wasn't part of the deal. This place isn't all that dirty. Why don't you just take a break? Have a seat?"

The twisted man saluted and jeered, sat down on the floor, right in the spot where he had swept all the dirt.

"The boy is an idiot," the old man said. "You can't take any of his lies to heart. He doesn't mean them, not as lies anyway, because he has no idea what is real and what is just in a storybook that his mother might be reading to him. Look about? Is she here? And if she's here, what page is she on?"

"No one is here but me and your grandson, or perhaps your great-nephew, sir."

"Oh? Vilem is here? Tell him to turn the storybook to the tale of the Wolf Magician. It is quite my favorite of all time."

"No, uncle! It is I, Wasilly!"

"The cripple? Why aren't you hanging from a post, wriggling your legs to distract the wolves when the shepherds return the sheep to fold?"

"You are such a mean old fool! They stopped all that non-sense when I was nine years old!"

"Wasilly," said the old man. "I have something to ask of you."

"Yes?"

"Will you turn to the story of the Wolf Magician and read it to me? My eyes aren't so good, or I'd do it myself. Do so at my behest."

Leonard saw that the room was entirely bare of books.

"Oh, all right," the hunchback said with a sigh. "There was once a time, upon which there were two orphans. A big one and... also... a smaller one. The big one was called Mendark, and the little one, Pigneisis. They both had faces, but they didn't look the same otherwise. Neither of their faces was very attractive, and both would be marked ugly on the census forms. This is not to say that they were ugly after the same fashion! No, not all! One had buggy eyes and a nose like a car-rot. The other had lips like onions and ears like moustaches."

"Which was which?" the old man asked.

"Er, Mendrek had the carrot nose, and Pigensus had the onion moustaches. As I was saying, they were both in dire need of entertainment one day as they sat in their barren hovel, which they shared together after the death of their respective wives, who were both now dead four years and buried near rivers, two different ones."

"Which rivers?"

"Er, Maldrake's wife was buried by the Heinclasm River. The other, by the Skeinvart."

"I've never heard of those."

"I shouldn't wonder. They are in strange and distant lands. Now shall I continue with the story?"

"Why do these orphans have wives?" Leonard said.

"Well, they grow up, don't they?"

"Then why even mention that they were orphans?" Leonard continued. "Does it play into the tale at all? I mean, is there a portion where they lament, 'If only our parents hadn't died when we were children, perhaps we wouldn't be sharing a hovel and relying on a Wolf Magician to entertain us!' Is it something along those lines?"

Through gritted teeth, the hunchback spat, "I didn't write the foolish story! I'm only reciting it for my grandfather, you... stupid soldier!" He rose, wobbled, nearly toppled, and then staggered from the room, slamming the thin, rickety door on exit.

"Who is that boy, your grandson or your nephew?" Leonard asked the old man after a moment.

"He's a sheep turd," the old man growled. "Thank you for driving him away. Now I can really get some gardening done."

——◦——

The ground was pale gray, almost like slushy snow, though winter had yet to come. Inside the gloomy hovel, there was little but a stove, a chair, and a pile of rags that Captain Kaspar took to be a bed. He asked the peasant woman, "Could you tell me where the girl is now? I really should like to take a look at her."

"I think she needs a doctor, sir, not a soldier."

"I'm a highly trained officer. I know some of medicine, as well as a little about many other things. And in any case, she may need a priest more so than a physician."

"You are neither a priest, nor a physician," she said, rising and pointing to the back door.

"But I was a novice in a monastery before I went to officer's school. It is there I acquired my knowledge of witching matters."

"Whoever told you Miglė had anything to do with witching? My daughter suffers from a goiter, sir. I suspect you have been misinformed."

"Goiters are the easiest place to hide," he said, rather gruffly.

The woman rolled her eyes, then led Captain Kaspar to a shed used recently as a chicken coup until its conversion into a sick room for the young Miglė. She lay there sleeping in a filthy nightshirt. She was an entirely normal girl of nine, apart from a growth the size of a muskmelon that extended from the back of her neck.

"Well, well, well. I can assure you this is no goiter."

"How's that?"

"You don't get goiter on the back of the neck. This... this is something else. Leave me with her."

The woman hesitated a moment, then turned and departed, closing the flimsy door as she went.

"Miglė, my girl, are you awake?" Captain Kaspar said, bending close and inspecting the tumorous thing.

The girl's eyes opened, and she turned her head slightly to see the stranger hovering above her.

"Don't be afraid. I am here to help with your... your problem. May I touch your neck for a moment?"

She gave no reply. Slowly, he reached out and placed his palm on the protuberance, finding it warm and feeling a faint pulsing from within. He sensed the small spastic motions of a baby kicking within its mother's womb.

"You are a lucky little girl," he told her. "You have been chosen for a very special purpose. I'm going to have to do one teensy little thing that might cause you discomfort, so sit up for a minute and drink this." He pulled a flask of strong spirits from his coat.

She took a sip and began hacking violently. "It tastes like poison!" she cried.

"No, it's not poison. It's a kind of medicine. If you just have three more sips, you'll be okay."

"The bump will go away?"

"Well, not yet. But it will let me see exactly what kind of bump this one is. Then later, I can make the bump go away."

She gagged down a few more swigs of the liquor and handed the flask back.

He told her a story of three brass dwarves who found a black swan swimming in an open grave during heavy rain, giving the alcohol a chance to take effect. Her eyes grew heavy and bleary, and he told her to lie down and to try and relax.

He pulled his bayonet from his boot. The incision was small, fast, and deep. Blood oozed forth, but it was black and viscous like the blood of a man dead several hours. He reached in his index finger and yanked it back quickly in surprise. Gripping the tip was a tiny, gnarled hand.

"Excellent," he said. "Let's get you into town."

Zaba stood back and scratched his head. "Wouldn't you know it? There are two boxes."

"Of course," said Meinrad, brushing dirt from the ebony box. "Did you think this was all a joke?"

Vilmas dragged the second box from the hole and let it rest beside the first.

"One is black, and one is silver," Myska said. "I am surprised the silver one is not tarnished."

"It's obviously not true silver," Jezek said.

"That's a shame. We could sell it," Zaba said.

"The captain wouldn't be too happy if you did," Meinrad said.

"I mean," Zaba said, "if it's the wrong box. The other box, of course."

"You fools don't even realize what he wants the boxes for, do you?" Vilmas said. He was sitting on the ground, finally resting and wiping the sweat from his face and brow with a rag. "He wants them both. But he doesn't want you jackasses getting any big ideas about opening them. So he tells you one is a bad box, which it is, but maybe not in the way you think."

"They are not big enough to be proper coffins," Zaba said. "They are the size of, perhaps, baby coffins."

"I'm telling you, they house cats," Jezek said with a chuckle.

"So," said Zaba. "Sergeant Leonard is with the old man, and Captain Kaspar is looking in on the little girl. Then where are Lieutenants Moser and Gruber? Do you know this, Ensign Meinrad?"

"I don't think I am at liberty to divulge that right now, men."

"It's all right if you don't know. You can admit it," Vilmas said.

"That's enough antagonism from you, corporal. Let's all just take a break and wait for the captain. Jezek will fetch us food and drink. Here's a Krone."

Jezek took the coin and asked, "Is there something in particular you'd like me to bring back?"

"Cheese," chittered Myska.

"Sausages," croaked Zaba.

"Wine," groaned Vilmas.

"How about as much bread and beer as that Krone will get you," Meinrad suggested. "Perhaps apples if they can be got cheaply."

"Apples are for horses," Vilmas said, and spat into the air overtop Myska's head.

"You foul beast!" Myska screeched, wiping his face with his sleeves.

"Corporal, don't you have anything better to do?" Meinrad asked.

"Aye, aye, sir," the large man said, pulling a little flat tin from his pocket. Opening it, he revealed five golden cigars.

"Is that... Angel Hair?" Zaba said, eyes wide.

"Only the finest," Vilmas assured them. He removed one and proffered it to the ranking officer. Meinrad gladly accepted.

<hr />

Gruber and Moser huddled together, pulling the blankets tightly around themselves to shield their bodies from the freezing winds coming off the frozen sea. Their heads were hooded, with cloths pulled against their faces into which only eyeholes had been cut. Neither had gloves, so they both wore socks over their hands to keep their fingers from becoming so brittle that they might simply snap and fall away. Moser had been entrusted with the crystal they'd fetched, and he kept it in a small purse affixed to his belt. The men perched there on the precipice, overlooking the chunks of greenish-blue salt ice.

"What ship could possibly navigate these waters?" Moser said, but he couldn't be heard above the roar of the winds.

"Is it noon?" Gruber said, looking at the solid gray sky. There was no way to tell where the sun was positioned. Each man had a rather nice pocket watch, which had frozen.

"We can't hold out much longer. Either the ship arrives, or we freeze to death when the sun sets."

"I'm sorry I can't help the two of you survive here," said a snowman, his teeth acorns, his nose a parsnip, his eyes bits of shale. "Meatmen just aren't designed to weather our climes. I really do hope the ship is on time."

"Yours are a noble and generous people, Aniko," Gruber said. "We will never forget all you have done. But now, my comrade and I must die."

"All right, if you must," Aniko said, disappointed. He raised his broom-spear in the form of a salute.

"Well, I suppose we could wait a bit longer... see if the ship arrives?" Moser said, hopefully. There were icicles in his moustache that broke off as he added, "I'm really in no hurry to be dead."

"I can wait," agreed Gruber. "The sea certainly is tumultuous." Ice drifts pushed forth onto the frozen shore, flowing like languid waves.

"I can't imagine what kind of ship rides these hoary waters," Moser said.

"A ship of diamond," Aniko said. "Wrought in the ancient times by mystic craftsmen who were half god. Diamonds are the ice of the gods. They use them to cool their drinks when the weather becomes hot, as I hear it does in other lands."

"Where will the ship take us?" Moser asked.

"We snowmen do not really know, for we never go there. But we sing songs about the place. In the old tales that our grandparents heard as children, the place is called Earth, and it is thought to be home to not only meatmen, but also birds and fish and beasts of meat, as well."

"Yes, we need to go back to Earth," Gruber said. "I hope the ship can take us there, though I can't see how it could."

"Don't you yet know that the diamonds are the stars?" Aniko said. "They keep the sky cool at night. The sky is the gods' swimming pool. They like the brisk feeling of cold water on the skin, to keep them young, they say. Wake them up."

"We can sail on a falling star back to Earth?" Moser asked.

"If you are particularly lucky, then, yes, I think so," said Aniko.

Both men frowned, for Moser had particularly good luck, always landing on his feet, and Gruber had particularly bad luck, always landing butter-side down. They knew, without a doubt, that they would cancel each other out, giving them perfectly average luck, which meant they would crash to their deaths on a giant diamond, if the diamond even showed up before they died of exposure.

"Luck is like the gods' money," Aniko explained. "Some people are born rich and others, poor. There is no rhyme or reason to luck, just like there is none to the economy. A meatman wants a loaf of bread, it might cost him twelve hundred Kronen. Another meatman wants a loaf of bread, it might cost him only a Heller. That's how valuation occurs in your crazy world, gentlemen."

"Do not blame me for mercantilism or monetary policy," Gruber said over the rush of icy waves lapping at the cliff. "I am a man of the sword, by which I had always thought to die. But now, I shall die by the sea, it seems."

"I suppose I could stab you both to death if you think it would be kinder," the snowman said. He pointed the sharpened broomstick at Moser and gave a mock jab.

"No call for that," Moser said. "When the time comes, we shall jump to our deaths, good friend."

"Alas, we know not what time it is," Gruber said. He hung his head and shivered. "I think that time is frozen as solid as our watches, and it no longer marches forward, unlike the ice flows, working their way up this crag. Moser, I tell you, we may not even have to jump. The ice will crush and smother us, and we will join it as a pink current, returning to the deep on the tide."

"Our blood is as salty as this frosty brine," Moser mused, in between the chattering of his teeth. "We are but escapees from an aquatic prison, with tubes of the stuff still circulating within us. Now we are the seawater's prisons. Its brothers are coming to set it free."

"It is clear that you are both delirious and in shock," Aniko said. "It won't be long now, my dear friends. Shall I proceed with the stabbing?"

"Our doom is as clear as the diamond ship that has not arrived to pick us up," Gruber murmured.

Moser smirked. "What I like about you, Gruber, is that you never know when you are wrong."

And they began to rise into the sky. Or rather, a portion of the ground on which they stood broke free of the surrounding cliff and took them with it, sailing up and out over the icy ocean.

"Is that where old men go when they die?" rasped the bedridden man. His breaths were now irregular. Leonard had begun to worry.

"I'm not sure I understand the question, sir," Leonard replied.

"If I died in battle, as a young fighting man, I would surely go to the hall of those northern gods, but as I am old and enfeebled, I will die a coward's death and be sent to live in a frozen pit."

"I know you've got plenty of fight left in you yet," said Leonard, staring out the window.

"Your friends, sergeant... are they all right?"

"I suppose so. Which ones?"

"The ones who were freezing to death. Did they make it home?"

Leonard spun to look at the old man, quite annoyed by the absurdity of the question. "Why are you asking me?"

"Is that not why you are here, dear Leonard? To tell an old man stories by the side of his sickbed?"

"I am here because I am a soldier on guard. Any additional indulgences occur purely at my pleasure, sir."

"But you are such a good storyteller. So much better than my grandsons and nephews. Tell me a story. Please?"

The soldier turned slowly, made his way to the bed, and sat. He said to the old man, "Once, when I was a boy, I was taken to a little island in a large lake where ponies lived. In the process of being sold to another owner across the lake, a ship sank many years before, and the surviving ponies swam to that island where they were really quite successful but too much trouble to round up. Now they live there, as wild as can be. And as a child, I was very excited to see these small horses, and I assumed I could ride them. But as soon as we disembarked the ferry, I saw a hand-painted sign that said, 'Wild Ponies Bite and Kick.' After that, I gave up on dreams."

"Oh, I don't buy that for one minute. You must be remembering it wrong."

"Well, there is another incident I recall. My younger sister, probably six at the time, was learning to write. We had a slate that she practiced upon. And one day, the slate disappeared without any trace. A few months later, I found the slate hidden in the pigsty. Though dirty, I could still see the crudely scrawled phrase, 'I love my Grammy, I love my Grammy,' written over and over, probably twenty times."

"What did it mean? Is that what she called your grandmother?"

"I have no idea. Both our grandmothers were long dead before she was even born."

"Was it even written by your sister?"

"I can't be sure. I like to think it was, because I found that slate shortly after she was pecked to death by the geese. They became really violent that autumn."

When the wolves arrived, it was night, and Leonard had begun to doze off. He could hardly be sure of what he was witnessing. The moonlight streamed in through the window near the old man's sickbed, illuminating the scene with that unbelievable shade of blue found only in dreams within dreams. A blue that madmen know well. At first, the elder coughed, nothing out of the ordinary. But the coughing grew louder until Leonard was jarred fully awake. He cautiously approached the bed, leaving his musket leaning against the wall.

"Sir?"

"Leonard," the man gasped. "Are there wolves?"

That fragile and aged body racked with violent fits. The dry coughing became wet, and from that toothless maw appeared the first sign of the long-awaited wolves. At first, Leonard was not sure what it was that protruded from the man's mouth. It was dark, slimy, and covered in fur. A paw? The tip of the muzzle? The first wolf had begun to emerge.

It was too soon, the soldier feared. The others had failed to accomplish their tasks, and the wolves would surely escape. The doors in the shack too flimsy to withstand them, the fence full of holes. At one time, that tall fence and its hexes prevented the passage of the beasts. That was a long time in the past. If worst came to worst, he would simply have to shoot them. But what then? The captain had not told him what would happen if even one of the wolves was killed.

The second began to break forth, rupturing the old man's hand like the popping of a balloon. Another bloody appendage emerged. A tongue poked out and began licking at the blood. The wolf snapped its teeth and yelped as it struggled to be free of its impossibly small container. The man's arm roiled and bubbled with the undulations of the hairy monsters within. A gash appeared in the man's chest, and the entire body of a beast leapt out, flinging gore upon the awestruck sergeant's face and uniform.

A howl pierced the night. Deafening Leonard. He backed toward the wall, feeling for his musket. His bayonet ready in his other hand.

The old man's body was now bloody rags being worried by the jaws of the newly freed pack. Seven or eight, Leonard could not keep track. Then the animals turned to Leonard and they sang of one voice that was still many: "Where is she? Where is she? Let us tarry not, but show us to her. Find us the virgin, sir. For what big teeth we have."

———◆———

There were two boxes. There was a little girl. There was a crystal. There were a few Austrian officers, some Bohemian enlisted men, and a large Hungarian guzzling beer and eating bread and apples. It was a regiment recruited for special missions, and now they sat together in the torch light outside a rundown house that belonged to what was once the most powerful man in that countryside. He had long ago been afflicted with the wolf plague foretold in songs that children sang back when men spoke languages no one even remembered the names of. And now they had the girl with the witch living in her neck. They had the good and the bad box. And they had the crystal from the World of Ice.

"We are ready," Kaspar told his men. "Only let us hope that Leonard has kept this situation contained. If he loses even one wolf...." He trailed off, but the men weren't listening to hear it.

Vilmas, looking rather dashing all done up in his uniform, took up a great hammer and smashed down the door to the house in one blow. Even as the splinters were flying, the first wolf pounced, knocking the large man to the ground and tearing at his throat. Zaba rushed forward and swatted the beast with the stock of his musket, though it was clear the great Hungarian bastard was beyond help.

"We have the girl!" Kaspar called from atop a hay cart. He lifted her, her tiny limbs flailing in terror so that the beasts could gaze upon her and understand that there was no trickery or trap this time. Things were going according to the prophecy. This time.

The rest of the wolves rallied with their comrade outside the house. Behind them staggered Leonard, his left arm wrapped in his coat.

"Did they savage you, sergeant?" Meinrad asked.

"Not exactly. I had to cut off pieces of my flesh to toss to them and keep them occupied until you all arrived." And then he showed the men his wounds. In the torch light, his arm looked like a picked rabbit carcass. A dead horse leg.

"We ate the members of the household," the wolves sang, "and we are not sated. They were a lame and dim-witted lot. Full of nothing but woe and blubber. Give her to us! Give her to us!"

"Come forward, wolf friends," the captain called to them.

The girl began to shriek and kick the man with her spindly legs.

The wolves gathered, their leader howling some eerie diminished chord. They padded forward in lockstep.

Jezek stood to one side of the captain, holding one of the boxes draped in grimy linen. Meinrad whipped the cloth away, revealing the black box. He flipped the lid open, and Gruber shoved the crystal inside.

A crack. The snapping of necks. The firing of a pistol. The dropping of a stoneware jug. The breaking of dry boughs. All these sounds lived within that crack. It was spoken by the black box but was repeated by the echoes of every surface in the countryside. The trees were babbling their crackle to the hills. Bats were sent into nose dives, confused by the alteration of the sonic landscape. A few farms over, a baby woke, screaming for its mother.

The wolves knew that crack too well.

"You did it again! You woke her! You did it again!" they sang, both in contempt and dismay. "Every time we live this time, it is the same, again and again. But we know what we must do!"

The lead wolf charged the captain directly, and the others scattered, flanked, ran serpentine, leapt over the hay cart, or doubled back.

"Chaos!" cried Myska, holding back one of the beasts with his musket.

"It is written!" screamed Captain Kaspar. He sliced into the girl's neck mass, just as the wolf leader pounced on him. But the cut was large enough for the witch to emerge from her hibernation, awakened fully by the Cracking of Time. She crawled out as a shriveled thing the size of an infant, wrinkled skin coated in a fine, downy hair. The next second she was the size of a sheep, and the down had sprouted into cinereous feathers. Her face became that of a black lion as she grew to the size of an adult and then further. Before two heartbeats passed, she towered over the wolves and men alike, skin as white as pride, gaunt as famine, dressed in the gown of a Russian noblewoman.

Leonard, dazed and fading, regarded his stripped arm bones, then looked to the Winter Witch, and then saw the wolves flinch, if only for a moment. The crisis point reached, all would be decided in the next breath. Would things play out as they always did, or would destiny deviate this time? He wondered this aloud, but at such a low volume that none of his comrades could hear him, not that they would have paid him any mind if they had.

Captain Kaspar rose, slightly battered, and gave a signal with his saber.

Moser scrambled to the side of the ghastly and mystifying woman. But was careful not to approach too closely, because the woman could breathe death into the very air. Her breath was so cold it could freeze a man dead, and she leaned down toward the pack leader, who gripped the bleeding girl in his teeth and dragged her backward, away from his newly hatched adversary.

"There are no windows in the center of a room," she said without speaking.

The wolf worried at the moribund child in his maw as he slunk away. The rest of the pack took on a submissive stance. Fight or flight?

Leonard shouted, "You have me inside you now, you bastards! You have my flesh inside you!"

"Shut up!" said Zaba, still standing guard by their fallen brother.

Then the Winter Witch sobbed, or so it seemed. Her chest heaved, and a force broke its way free of her mouth, leaving a trail of frosty ether in its wake. An arm of frozen magic scooped the lead wolf up, causing the girl to slip free of its bite. The wolf was squeezed and bent by invisible hands, whimpering only briefly, before it was shaped into a ball of gray hair, no blood or tearing, no sign of ever having been anything else but a ball. And that ball was sent hurtling toward the remaining pack, who were now paralyzed by fear and indecision, like a game of bowls. Each wolf hit by the hairy ball was knocked into the silver box that Moser held up at the witch's side, and then the ball zagged to the next. And though Leonard, a skilled billiards player, couldn't see that the angles made any sense, or how the wolves could all fit into a box the size of an infant coffin, he watched them become trapped once again in the box that he would have to keep with him for the rest of his days. Moser called for Leonard to close the box, which he did with his remaining whole arm.

It was over. It had all happened so quickly that Leonard regretted carving up his own arm. Because he knew it meant that he was damned now, and he was really going to miss that arm.

The Winter Witch, snarling, snatched away the black box from Jezek. She broke it against a rock and recovered the crystal from within.

The men, rightly afraid of this entity, backed away from her, maintaining eye contact. They bowed in unison.

She pointed at the girl, now dead.

"Do not let this happen again," she said. Gripping the crystal tightly, she jetted into the night sky, leaving a trail of stardust.

"That is the most truly terrifying thing we ever face," Myska said. He collapsed on the ground, sprawled like a tired dog.

"It raises philosophical concerns," Zaba said, gaze locked on the corpse of Vilmas.

"What concerns?" Meinrad said.

"The usual ones I bring up now. Is the witch a lesser evil than the wolves? Et cetera. And then I point out how the wolves killed Vilmas so they can't be all bad. You know—gallows humor."

"And we all commiserate with Leonard now," said Captain Kaspar. "Because we know what he always faces next."

"That is true," Leonard said, toying with the bones of his dead limb. "But I know what I'm getting into every time this happens. I have no one to blame for my fate but myself."

"At first light we bury the girl and the Hungarian," said Moser or Gruber, it doesn't matter which. Sometimes it was one. Other times, the other.

⸺⬦⸺

Graves were dug with the speed and precision of men who had spent the entire previous day digging, minus the might of Vilmas, who had done the majority of the work by himself. Leonard's arm had been bandaged by Gruber, who had always wanted to train as a midwife but was prevented by the obvious sexual obstacle. Coffins were declared optional by Captain Kaspar after a thorough search of the house and outbuildings that turned up nothing of the sort. Zaba grunted a solemn tune.

"What is that you sing, Zaba?" Leonard asked.

"Ah," said the fat man, setting down his spade for a moment while Jezek, Meinrad, and Myska finished the second, larger grave. "It's a very old traditional song my grandmother would sing to me. *I Took One Apple to the Grave.*"

"Yes, it sounded familiar to me. Please, sing it louder so I can hear the words."

"I took one apple to the grave," Zaba began, loudly, soon joined by Myska and Jezek, "and I returned with a baby arm. One apple I did give the hairy boy I met along the way. I mistook him for a lapdog. He was an abomination. Heigh-ho!

Dark day when the maiden died. Into the hole, we put her now. Heigh-ho! Dark day, dark, dark day, dark day when the maiden died."

They ceased singing when the beating of horse-hoofs became louder than their chorus. A group of five English cavalrymen cantered up. The tall, burnsided leader, Major Hardmeat, called the others to a halt and then addressed Captain Kaspar: "Frightfully sorry so late, old chap. Held up by the French this time."

"We needed you here," Captain Kaspar said, burnishing his sword, not looking up, "to keep the wolves from escaping. As it stands, they could have just run away without the horses to keep them corralled."

"But they didn't escape, did they?" Hardmeat said.

"No! They didn't!" Moser said. "But they certainly could have!"

"Yes," agreed Meinrad, "I thought it was odd that the wolves didn't simply run away. But this explains it, then. The English cavalry were just delayed this time."

"We are usually here for the big confrontation," said Hardmeat's lieutenant, Clutterbuck, a rakish man with almost no chin. "Only thing stopping us was that for some reason our horses stopped."

"Refused to budge?" Meinrad said.

"No," Clutterbuck said with a frown. "Stopped being. They just *weren't*. Until a few hours ago when they just *were* again. And we got here as quickly as we were able."

"One minute we had horses," Hardmeat said. "The next, we didn't. And then, a few hours later, we had horses again. I had my secretary write it all down in detail. Problem is, there isn't all that much detail when your horses just cease to be. A distinct lack of detail, really, that leads one to wonder if all of existence is simply contingent upon the details that constitute it."

"I don't wonder such a thing," Leonard said.

"Is that right, sergeant? And why not?"

"I know exactly the nature of existence, and it precedes any possible description you could give of your horses not being there."

"That seems presumptuous," Hardmeat said, raising an eyebrow and removing a glove. "I suppose we should get on with the burials, eh?"

Zaba, Meinrad, and Jezek hauled Vilmas' heavy corpse to the hole. Myska pushed him in with his foot.

"If you are going to kick him in, at least make it a bit more ceremonious, lads," said the lank, blonde Captain Bonebrake. He beamed at them, perfect teeth giving away his privileged upbringing on distant Scottish estates.

Leonard stood next to the man, his arm in a sling. "How would one ceremoniously kick a dead body into a hole?"

"I don't know. They would recite one of their heathen blessings first, I shouldn't wonder."

Myska chittered something Leonard knew to be a laugh. "Holy Slavic spirits of ignorance! Please accept into the secret places of the Bohemian soil this foreigner. Sorrowfully, he was a Hungarian, which makes him a bastard and not even a Slav, but please see your way to forgiving him of his racial handicap. Take him to the spooky Underworld, where shades eat the ghosts of cabbage stew three times a day. Yours truly, Myska Danko."

Gruber carried the frail remains of the girl toward the other grave. He was stopped by Corporal Bracegirdle. The portly, middle-aged man said to Gruber, "Please, sir. It isn't right like this." He reached out tremulously and brushed a lock behind one of her delicate ears. "She needs to be washed. Her hair and her... body." He swallowed hard.

Unsure of how to proceed, Gruber eyed his commanding officer. "Sir?"

Captain Kaspar cleared his throat, folded his hands behind his back, and then slightly shuffled his feet. "Major Hardmeat, sir, I wonder if I could have a word with you in private."

Bracegirdle continued to fondle the girl's head and face, and whisper, "Wash her... wash her," as the two superiors retreated several yards from the others.

When they were sufficiently distanced, Major Hardmeat began to explain: "If this regards Bracegirdle's conduct, I can assure you—"

"Major, sir," interrupted the captain, "I don't mean to be impertinent, but do you really need all five of your men?"

"Why, captain, I don't quite understand."

"You see, it's only that there were supposed to be five of you all together. But instead, there are six, and at this late stage of exposition, I think four would really be more than enough to accomplish the task."

"Oh," the major said gravely, playing with his burnsides. "I can assure you I have only the most essential personnel."

"Who's the young boy?" Captain Kaspar said, pointing to a teenager gawking at the corpse of Vilmas.

"That's Young Glasscock. He... fetches and carries. He's our Jack-of-all-trades."

"And the fellow with the bushy moustache?"

"That's Pigfat. He's our doctor."

"Has he done anything yet to make himself important to the story?"

"Well, he did give medical attention to your sergeant. Dressed his wounds and put his arm in a sling."

"Oh, yes. Well, he must stay," said the captain with conviction. "That leaves Clutterbuck, Bonebrake, and Bracegirdle, who have already been introduced. As much as I hate to say it, we need to do without Bracegirdle and Young Glasscock. That should simplify matters a great deal."

The major scoffed and tossed his head back. "Well, you've got more men than I. And really—what's the purpose of having two lieutenants? Gruber and Moser are more or less interchangeable, aren't they? If you get rid of one of them, I'll get rid of Young Glasscock and Bracegridle." Then, speaking from the corner of his mouth, "Never had much use for that cretin Bracegirdle anyway."

"Well, if you are giving up two, I suppose I can do without Moser."

"Moser seemed more competent, in my opinion," the major offered.

"I'll thank you to leave me to manage the existence of my own men!" chided the captain.

"As you wish," Major Hardmeat said, and the two wandered back to their fellows.

Without much ado, Captain Kaspar approached Moser. The lieutenant looked at him with a quizzical grin. "Is everything quite alright, sir?"

"You are dismissed," the captain said imperiously.

The lieutenant's eyes widened. And he was no longer part of the story.

Major Hardmeat approached the young private called Glasscock. The boy seemed unsure of himself and pushed his hair out of his eyes. His bangs were far past regulation, but in a moment, none of that would matter.

"Dear, dear Glasscock," the major said, "let me have a look at you." He grabbed the boy's shoulders and pulled him closer, the young man jostling about like a sock monkey. "You are a fine lad, truly." And he embraced the boy, holding him tightly.

Glasscock tried to pull away.

"I love you lad, but Hardmeat crushes Glasscock!" And he squeezed until the boy was no longer there.

"Major, sir!" cried Bonebrake, "who's going to fetch and carry?"

"Are you questioning my decision to eliminate Young Glasscock?"

"Sir?" Bonebrake said, with terror in his face.

"I can fetch and carry, sir," the fat Bracegirdle said. "I don't mind one bit."

"No, you rotund oaf!" roared the major. "You can't fetch or carry, because you don't *exist*."

And the major was right. Bracegirdle didn't exist.

Without interference, Gruber delicately laid the body of the girl in her grave.

"Should we keep going?" Jezek wondered, feigning business.

"Oh, I almost forgot about you, Jezek," Captain Kaspar said. And the man vanished from the tale, retroactive to the beginning. "We can just assume all his tasks were completed by, I don't know, Myska."

"Oh, captain, that seems like a lot more work for me," Myska said.

"Very well. Split the workload with Zaba."

"But, sir," protested the fat man, "we are now the only two remaining Bohemians here! Can't we at least have a pet dog called Ohař? Can't he have a handkerchief tied around his neck?"

"Oh, I'll allow it," the captain said with a wave of the hand.

A Blenheim mongrel ran from the bushes, barking.

"Ohař!" cried Myska and Zaba.

Everyone was very happy for a moment. The hardened military men were overwhelmed with the feeling that a heart is filled with upon seeing two men reunited with their faithful canine who had just come into existence. They gave out *awwws* and *mys*, and a few men applauded. The two massaged the hound's croup and withers.

Then everything was just as it should be. That was the end.

———◇———

The old man shifted in his bed. "Bullshit! Bullshit!" he groaned, his voice a tatter of its former self. "This story is going nowhere. You aren't telling it right!"

The soldier sat forward and glared at the bedridden codger. "You wanted me to tell you a story, didn't you? That's what I'm doing. I'm telling you a story."

"You have to get it right! Make the story right!" shouted the old man.

A loud knock came at the frail door to the bedroom.

"Sergeant Wolf!" came the voice from behind the thin, clattering slats of wood. "Is my grandfather in need of help?"

"No," Wolf said. "Mr. Leonard is quite all right. He's just confused by my story. That is all."

"Oh, I see. Could Jiri come in to sweep?"

"Not right now. Cleaning can wait until tomorrow."

The soldier sat on a silver box about the size of an infant coffin. He said to the old man lewdly, "I bet in your day, it was acceptable to rape the women in the villages you took."

"No. It was not acceptable, but it did happen on occasion," the old Leonard rasped. He panted inhumanly. "I don't know what's happening now. I feel like I'm about to spread open and infect the world."

"That's why I'm here, old man. Leave it to me."

"Sometimes, I hear what the wolves say to me."

"And what do they say?"

"They tell me that I took one apple to the grave of the maiden. I cannot for the life of me recall having an apple that day. Years later, I saw Meinrad, who had been promoted to captain, and he gave a solemn oath that I had taken an apple to her grave. The group had eaten hard-crust sour bread and apples earlier in the day. Zaba had given one to me. And since it was in the song, I went ahead and took one apple to the grave."

"Would Meinrad have any reason to lie?"

Leonard, skin thin as tissue paper, breath strained as water through a sieve, said, "I can't see where Meinrad had any reason to do anything. Fate is fate. Destiny is destiny." He coughed, rattling his body and bloodying the sheets. When the fit stopped, he said, "The next time, I'll remember to take the apple. If there's one thing I've learned in life, it is this: there will always be wolves. You can eliminate your Jezeks and your Bracegirdles. Moser and Gruber might be interchangeable.

The cavalry may or may not arrive on time. But there will always, always be wolves. So there should always be an apple."

Sergeant Wolf stared out the wavy glass window. The fog substantially obscured his vision so that he could see only an apple tree, and next to it, a small headstone, tossed up at a sharp angle by the roots. In that space, there was a profound absence of wolves.

And yet, there were wolves.

I TOOK A CHEMTRAIL AT TACO BELL AND NOW I DEAD

Sometimes it's 1979.

Sometimes it is. Most times it is not. It was once, though.

And somewhere in the world, a young boy named Konrath waited to fulfill his destiny.

I can vaguely remember it...

I. NineTeenSevenTeeNine

"Women don't like a man who doesn't know what year it is," Vince tells me. "I'm going to get ice cream." He wanders into the kitchen and spoons out a large bowl.

My Sharona is playing on the radio. I imitate the bass line with my mouth.

"It's one of the greatest riffs ever," says the window washer, hovering outside our apartment window on his lift. He really should be minding his own business. I close the window and the blinds because I'm totally naked. Not even socks on, not even any band-aids.

"That guy is creepy," says Vince, adjusting his tanned human-skin mask so that he can get the spoonfuls of ice cream into his mouth. "I can't wait for Texas Chainsaw Massacre II to come out," he says in between bites.

"Dude, it's 1979. That won't be out for seven more years," I tell him.

"What's the longest anyone has waited for a sequel?"

"How long was it between the Old Testament and the New Testament?" the window washer yells so we can hear him.

He has a point. But then, I think: "Hey, what about the Book of Mormon?"

"That was such bullshit!" the window washer says, waving his squeegee erratically. "I was looking forward to seeing how G-d topped NT and it was such a freaking let down. You can't end on *Revelation* and then pull this lost tribe bullshit for the sequel."

"There's no way I'm reading the next one," Vince says.

I hear the toilet flush. My super-sexy girlfriend, Shana, is finally done in there. She strolls out, wearing her blue Cookie Monster-eye t-shirt she got at Super Waltonbauer's.

"You can't wear that shirt in 1979," I tell her.

"Oooh, I like a man who knows what year it is," she says, slowly pulling the t-shirt over her head, exposing her breasts and her tummy, which is so cute I just want to eat it up.

"Tummy play is going to be big this year," I tell her, placing my hand on the small abdominal mound and giving it a wiggle.

"Gross, I'm still eating my ice cream," says Vince, adjusting the dead-skin mask, making it harder for him to see. "I'm just imaging that her stomach is a huge balloon filled with milk now."

"My stomach is not huge!" she cries.

"Darling, it is rather bigger than most party balloons," I point out in my 1876 accent, and she concedes, for she does not wish me to think her a hysteric.

Roxanne comes on the radio.

"Fuck yeah, this is my jam!" screams the window washer, sloshing his bucket of cleaning fluid all over his feet.

"You can't say that yet. It's 1979," I remind him.

"Oh, I mean, I gotta boogie!"

Shana whispers to me, "I don't like that guy. I don't think he knows what year it is."

"But I know it's 1979, so I'm getting laid this year," I say and kiss her forehead. She tastes like soap. But that's fine. It's better to be clean in 1979 than dirty in 1876.

Another girl I know named Ramona comes in so that this story can pass the Bechdel Test.

"Hi, Shana," she says. "What's your favorite thing about 1979?"

Shana thinks for a minute. "The Oil Crisis."

"Mine too," Ramona says. "Or maybe ABBA."

"I think the TV of 1979 is great," Vince says, turning the set on with a giant remote control-box connected to the set by a long cable. "Look how square it is."

Ramona turns off the radio, which has just begun to play *Heart of Glass*, an obvious coded warning about the influence of CHEMTRAIL. (Several types of CHEMTRAIL can literally transmogrify a subject's heart to glass.)

"Is Konrath's speech on?" Shana asks.

"Oh, look!" I say. "It's our favorite made-for-television Sci-Fi Western!"

We all take our seats to enjoy the era-appropriate television content—even the window washer.

II. Electric Thunder

The sky was full of robots. A beautiful day, their contrails streamed boldly, painting the sky in a modernistic style. This was not surprising. Robots considered themselves to be highly modern—advanced even. They didn't give a shit about the boots on the ground.

The boots on the ground belonged to LeRoy Jaxwell, King of Cowboys, scepter-slinger.

They were ostrich-skin cowboy boots, bedecked in diamonds and conch pearls that, while naturally pink, were painted mannish-blue by some artisan living in utmost integrity behind the old pile of burlap sacks the potato-maker tossed into the alley.

LeRoy Jaxwell, King of Cowboys, gazed up in enchantment.

"Never seen no bots behavin' theyselfs so nice-like," he said to his entourage, consisting mainly of preteen ballerinas and sad clowns coated in thick paraffin.

"Yes, yes, yes," the lot of them chattered back. One of the sad clowns reached to touch the back of the cowboy's hand while he wasn't looking, then thought better of it and simply snapped a selfie at a clever angle that made it appear he was dwarfing LeRoy, a man of no less than seven feet tall.

The selfie was a lie. And the television announcer reminded you that it was 1979, and no one knew what a self was yet. This is, after all, science-fictional.

Oblivious, LeRoy gasped and cried out, "One day, I'm-a gonna turn me into a robutt and go a-flyin' up there with the best of 'em!"

"Yes, yes, yes," his cadre of hangers-on agreed.

"So where are we with that?" LeRoy said sternly to the young ballerina he had appointed head of R&D.

"Roboticization?" she asked, doing a pirouette.

"Yes, when can I get me all robofied? I wanna shoot round the sky like a pinball!"

"I'll need a little time in the lab to work out the kinks, my lord," she said in the first position.

"Labs are for nerds, li'l gal. The only lab we need is the lab of reality."

"Well," she said hesitantly, "I could work a lot faster if we had some funding... say, from CHEMTRAIL."

"CHEMTRAIL?" said the cowboy, putting his hand to his chin in contemplation. "It would go against my politics fer sher. People should be killed by the sky robutts all natural, with lazers and lazer swords—not by chemicals. On the other hand, I would compromise all my principles and get way above my raisin' if'n it let me be a sky robutt! Let's do it!"

A six-foot-three man—whom you might describe as tall were it not for his proximity to LeRoy—in a black business suit and even blacker shades shouldered past the pathetic retinue and introduced himself: "I'm Lawrence Hadron-Collider, representative of Big CHEMTRAIL out of San Jose. Here's my card." He handed a card to LeRoy that read: "I'm Lawrence Hadron-Collider, representative of Big CHEMTRAIL out of San Jose. Here's my card."

LeRoy looked it over carefully and silently mouthed the words "I can't read." Fade to black.

You usually fast-forward through the commercial break, but this time you decide to watch the one for Big CHEMTRAIL. It's just a single camera shot of a moderately attractive woman in great shape running up a hill. She's wearing a shirt that says "SHUT UP AND DANCE" and black yoga pants. A voice-over explains the side effects as the woman runs past the top of the hill and into the sky, becoming a stream of CHEMTRAIL. It is simply stunning. You aren't sure if they give awards for commercials, but this sure deserves one if they do.

When the show returns, you see two middle-aged, plus-size black women sitting on a bench outside a supermarket, evidently on their work break. Somehow you recognize them as Big Jass and Lyl.

"You member as a kid," Big Jass said, "when you'd crush up all the leftover fortune cookies into a fine powder and snort it? We used to call that Chinese cocaine."

Lyl's eyes went wide as she chewed a mouthful of her chicken salad sandwich. "Girl, I thought we was talking about going to church."

"We was. That's where we used to do the most Chinese cocaine."

"What church was you going to as a girl?"

"It was the Korean Methodist church coupla blocks over. We didn't *go there* go there. We just went there to do Chinese cocaine with the little boys. It didn't work unless you sniffed it right off the end of a peewee."

"We ain't did nothing like that at my church," Lyl said. "We was God-fearing people. Spent most of the time hiding behind the pews lest the Lord see us in our naked and wretched state."

"But you did Chinese cocaine at some point in your youth, right? At least dabbled in it?"

"No, ma'am. Ain't never touched the stuff. Chinese marijuana about as far as we went. That's when you take a CHEMTRAIL and lace it with dried bok choy. Learned about it in a Korean restaurant."

"I heard that old Arthur Bremer boy was hopped up on Chinese marijuana when he shot Wallace a few years back."

"Probably right. That why he forgot to shout out 'A penny for your thoughts' before he shot the man. Never sure why he chose that catchphrase, though."

"I guess that's funny," Jassy said, "because the shell casings is copper like a penny."

"Oh, I never even thought of that. That *is* pretty funny!"

And they both laughed and laughed and laughed. Lyl covered her mouth, but a little bit of half-chewed chicken salad slid down the side of her face, causing Big Jass to laugh even louder.

They laughed so loud and long that the Laugh Police came to arrest them, and they both continued laughing at the patrolman's ponytail, so he tazed them, which just gave them super electro-powered laughter that shook the very ground and sky, and they could not be stopped. Their chuckles stunned hummingbirds, and their guffaws brought down CHEMTRAIL jets. They are still on the loose to this day. Please call this number if you see either of them: XXX-5%5-1234.

III. The Black Dawn of the Hairy Satans

One channel up, Lenny and Squiggy were taking turns banging Jack Tripper in the butt when Rerun burst into the apartment and shouted, "Shazbot!"

Squiggy fell to the floor, pants around his ankles, and cried miserably, "I'm so sorry, Rerun! I never meant to hurt you, lover! You are daddy's big boy. Jack means nothing to me."

"So typical!" Rerun yelled, charging toward his fallen paramour. "I brang you CHEMTRAIL straight from my homeworld, and this is how your white ass thanks me?"

"Hey, hey," Lenny cut in, making himself into an obstacle between the quarreling lovers, "this is a simple misunderstanding. I talked Squiggy into this! This is all my doing! If you want to a punch a honky, best be punching me!"

Jack was motionless, bent over the arm of the couch because he was just a Taiwanese sex robot created to get fucked, and his program had not yet been completed: Squiggy had yet to climax.

"Oh yeah, do right me," Jack said in his Cylon voice. "You bugger better than even the famous Buck Rogers who is known for his sexual prowess across the centuries."

"This motherfucker is a droid!" Rerun screamed. "I cannot even believe this shit. Squiggy, you broke my space heart. You know I'm jealous of androids!"

"I'm so sorry," the little greaser said, rising and pulling up his pants. "I just couldn't help myself."

Rerun pouted and dabbed at his eyes.

"Now how am I supposed to do my break dance routine tonight? I'm just too upset to do anything but sit around and eat ice cream and pound android behind."

"You're a hypocrite!" Lenny said, shaking a finger at the crying man.

"I'm just too upset to not be getting a robot hard-on."

"If you fuck Jack," Squiggy said supportively, "I will understand."

"Alright. Let me get to this." Rerun dropped his drawers just as Schneider walked in the still-open front door.

"Christ a-mighty!" Schneider said. "I just came over to grease the door hinges, but instead I think I'll use the grease on my man-sized dingus." He lubed up and masturbated as Rerun laid into Jack with the grace of a humping walrus.

"You know that greasy stuff is never gonna come off, Schneider," Lenny said, milling about, not sure who to fuck.

"As long as I come off, that's all that matters!" said the lewd handy-man. He squinted and made a fishy-face to signal his pleasure.

"I just feel so bad," Squiggy said. "I think I should probably go back to Milwaukee and kill myself."

"I'm fucking Jack Tripper!" Rerun grunted. "I'm fucking Jack Tripper!"

"Yes," replied Jack. "You are fucking me. Continue to fuck me."

"Motherfucker!" Dolemite rushed in, pushing Schneider to the ground. "Rerun, you stupid ass mother, we was supposed to be practicing our rap and break dance routine right now. You ain't got the time to be fucking this cracker robot. We got to get our act together. And I hope you don't mind, but I brought Arnold from *Happy Days* to teach us all a recipe."

The short restaurateur stuck his head through the doorway.

"Hi, Arnold!" said everyone.

"Hi, guys!" Arnold said with a grin. "I can't wait to teach all of you something about cooking today."

"I sure know I could use some pointers in the kitchen," Squiggy said, perking back up.

"You sure know how to cook in the bedroom, though, you little porcelain freak doll," Rerun said. Squiggy rushed to him, and they embraced gaily.

"Hey, man!" Dolemite said. "This is no time for tearful reunions. We got a rap and break dance routine to work out. One, two, three...."

Schneider pressed play on the ghetto blaster, and the opening strains of an instrumental version of Prince's *I Wanna Be Your Lover* rang forth.

Rerun went into full-on dance mode and everyone else clapped—on the 1 and 3 downbeats like a bunch of dumb honkies.

Dolemite began his characteristic brand of spoken word:

One day when I was on the street,

That fatso Rerun shuffled his feet,

And he came right up to me so sweet,

Said, "I got twenty kilos of CHEMTRAIL stuffed up my boypussy.

He's from another world, another time,

Where CHEMTRAIL is not hard to find,

And you can do so much you lose yo mind,

"Rerun," I say, "Show me what's up that boypussy."

People be tryin' to intervene,

But don't ever you try and get between,

Me and Rerun's boypussy,

Writing yo jive-ass articles in magazines.

Some say CHEMTRAIL will kill a brotha dead,

Or put insanity in yo head,

But I'm CHEMTRAILed up right now you see,

I been snortin' Rerun's boypussy.

You know you can smoke it too,

But you may not like what it does to you,

The Dawn of the Hairy Satans is overdue,

Coming from space with their deadly tattoos,

And the White Man will be singing the blues,

Like a CHEMTRAIL baby in a papoose,

Sun Ra can seem so obtuse,

When the Overseer is running the ruse.

So, you see me now and I'm bad as fuck,

I just waxed down my gold pick-up,

Driving round with CHEMTRAIL in the back you see,

That I got from Rerun's boypussy.

Rerun finished up a blazing headspin and stuck the landing in an amazing front split. The whole gang clapped so hard they had bruises on their hands the next day. Even Jack Tripper activated his mechanical klaxon alarm to announce his applause. It was totally sick.

"Whew!" Rerun said, standing up and toweling away his sweat. "I really worked up a big appetite."

"Just in time for me to show you how to cook something really great!" Arnold said. "I just need to grab something first."

He stepped outside the apartment door and wheeled in a large microwave on a wheeled stand.

"Oh no!" Lenny said, placing his hands on his forehead. "Not another robot! That's what got us into this mess to begin with!"

"Relax," Arnold replied. "This is a microwave oven. It cooks very fast."

"Only rich assholes and scientists have microwave ovens, Arnie," said Schneider. "It's 1979."

"Ah... well, this was the best recipe I could come up with. I was going to teach you all karate, but I can't for another five years. So you will have to settle for Arnold's Amazing Microwaved Mongolian CHEMTRAIL Chicken."

Rerun set up a small counter near the sofa for Arnold to demonstrate his recipe.

Lifting a dead, black bird that appeared to be covered in fur instead of feathers, Arnold began: "First you start with a Hairy Satan chicken, unplucked, that can be procured at your local Mongolian butcher shop."

Hot Lips Houlihan charged into the apartment. "You are all out of uniform! Stop this shameful display at once, or the colonel will hear of this!"

Hilarious bumbling hijinks ensued as everyone tried to rapidly get into fatigues for inspection. A zany brass soundtrack accompanied the fast-motion montage, which ended with Jack Tripper still bent over the arm of the sofa, but now in uniform with his drab trousers down around his ankles.

And then there was a commercial for a handheld electronic football game that looked kind of like a calculator but made harsh squaunching sounds, and two child actors pretended to find it very interesting until Mean Joe Greene appeared and started singing *I Love Trash* while he flapped his fuzzy green maw and bobbed his ping-pong ball eyes. The kids kicked his garbage can on its side and rolled him out of their bedroom and into a stadium where they handed him a CHEMTRAIL Cola and he went on to be a five-time All-Pro. This was widely regarded as one of the greatest commercials of all time while, conversely, the electronic football game just sat unused in a box of old toys that younger siblings would discover in the Eighties and then say, "What is this thing? A Geiger counter?"

IV: Now I Dead

Six days ago...

My friend was a hot French mime, and it worked out well because I did not speak French, and she did not speak. We were at Taco Bell.

Alvin Cole was there, standing by the east vestibule, with his beard that looked like the bristly facial hair of a peccary. He handed out some political literature to customers. I waved to him to let him know I recognized him, but he just widened his eyes and continued to give pamphlets to old ladies with trays full of Quesalupas.

The mime motioned exaggeratedly at Alvin, then made a silly face. I took this to mean she thought he was unattractive. Hot mimes are often superficially judgmental, but she thought I was hot enough to sit with at the Bell, so I just kept eating my chicken soft taco and intermittently trying to wave Alvin over to our table so that I could have an awkward conversation with a guy I went to high school with but haven't seen in twenty years.

After about the fifth beckoning, he finally approached with a quizzical look in his eye.

"Gary Gygax?" he said, sounding very unsure of himself, which is exactly how I remembered him in school.

"Close enough," I said. "How you been, Al?" I called him Al, though it felt unnatural, and I didn't recall whether he liked that nickname or not.

"I'm in politics now," he said and handed me a two-color brochure titled *I Took One CHEMTRAIL and Now I Dead* [sic], which was propaganda about joining the Anti-CHEM-TRAIL Party. "I'm the second-in-command. I work directly under Konrath."

My hot mime friend snatched the brochure away and began to tear it into tiny pieces, which she added to her confetti bag. She's the kind of mime who makes frequent use of confetti.

"Do they let you personally dismantle the jets?" I asked.

"Uh, no. Sometimes Konrath lets me edit the videos of all the CHEMTRAIL footage we receive from all over the world. I also get to modify the maps that track where the CHEM-TRAILing is heaviest that day. Spoiler alert: it's heaviest in Scranton, PA."

"Sounds like you do all the grunt work."

"I also get a free lunch if I come here to hand out literature for eight hours."

The mime did the international sign for "second-in-command my ass," but Al, evidently, could not read international signs. Then she made a silly face again and pointed at Al. He just rolled his eyes and looked away.

"Yeah," Al said awkwardly. "Sometimes I get to use my editing skills to enhance the footage. That's what I went to school for."

"For faking CHEMTRAIL footage?"

"No, not faking it. Sometimes the CHEMTRAIL just doesn't show up well on video because of the chemicals. The camera companies are all in bed with Big CHEMTRAIL. It's in the brochure." He smacked his lips and began to hand me another brochure. Then he looked at the hot mime and pulled it back into his stack.

"I'm glad you've done well for yourself," I said. I returned to eating my food, hoping he'd get the hint.

He stared at me for another minute before saying, "Well, these old ladies aren't going to bug themselves." He went back to standing by the vestibule like a creepy animatronic gorilla at a used car lot.

My friend mimed laughter hotly. I tried to shush her but felt foolish about it, so I took a sip of Baja Blast. Then she pulled a CHEMTRAIL from her purse and lit it up right there. I don't know if that is technically illegal since the government denies CHEMTRAIL exists, but it still seemed rude. None of the muumuu'd old ladies paid any mind. Several had finished their meals and moved on to chewing up the pamphlets Al had given them.

"Don't eat those. The ink is made from CHEMTRAIL," Al said meekly from across the restaurant.

My hot mime friend offered me a toke. I don't normally partake but she offered it in such a hot way that I could not refuse. I was hot for CHEMTRAIL, and I didn't care who knew it. I wanted Al to see, to know that everything he stood for was going up in smoke right before his eyes.

As I took the CHEMTRAIL and placed it between my lips, I became aware that Alvin Cole was filming me with his phone, muttering to himself that my death would finally be the one to open the world's eyes, because if people knew that Gary Gygax, creator of Dungeons & Dragons, was taken from them by CHEMTRAIL, they'd all demand an independent investigation and Konrath would finally be able to get a seat on the town council and really start to change the world.

"I'm not Gary Gygax," I said mutedly before coughing.

I coughed out my voice box first. Then my right lung. Then my spleen. Then something that looked like a hermit crab with no shell to hide in. Then I coughed out pure chemical sludge.

"I can't believe I'm getting all this," Al said. "Konrath is definitely going to have to promote me now!"

I wondered: how can someone be promoted higher than second-in-command? Once all the pure chemical sludge was coughed out, I coughed out impure chemical sludge. I coughed out a boiled shrimp. I coughed out my heart. The hot mime took the heart and put it in her drink cup full of ice so they could reattach it later.

But there was no later.

Now I dead.

BRONSON'S SHARK TANK

Bronson, the very rich American, arrived at his London flat accompanied by no fanfare after working and traveling 72 hours straight to promote his latest whatever. He was not greeted by Leeko and Kona, his sharks, who were not swimming in their shark tank. The tank, however, was not empty but filled with red-pink gelatin. Bronson angrily tossed his Komodo-skin briefcase (retail $25k) onto his sofa ($150k).

"I'm rich," he cried out. "How are people supposed to realize that if I don't have a tank full of sharks awaiting them upon entry to my apartment?" No one answered, mainly because there was no one else within earshot, but also because the question was rhetorical. He paced back and forth momentarily before approaching the enormous tank. He leaned over at an awkward angle to read a small, metallic label at its base. As quickly as he could, he dialed the assistance number provided on the label.

Ring, ring.

"Hello, this is Nigel speaking. How can I be of assistance today?" The tone of the Englishman's voice was pleasant even if distorted by cellular encoding and tiny speakers, which produced an effect not unlike two cans on the ends of a taut string.

"I'm having some trouble with my shark tank."

"Could you give me the model number, sir?"

He read again from the little label: "SRGST 5000."

"Ah, the Super-Rich Guy Shark Tank. Brilliant choice, sir."

"Well, I am super-rich," Bronson admitted abashedly, because this was within the dictates of the instructional book that wealthy Americans received upon arrival in London. Don't deny, just show some shame. "I am also American."

"Good choice on that part, too, sir. Canadian wouldn't have suited a fine gentleman like yourself. What seems to be the problem with your SRGST 5000?"

"My sharks are not in it. I came home from work, and my sharks have vanished."

"Is the tank empty then, sir?"

"No, it seems to be full of gelatin."

"Jelly is it, sir?"

Bronson pondered for a moment. "Yes... not jam. Jell-o, gelatin, jelly. Whatever you guys call it over here."

"And, if I may ask, what color is the jelly, sir?"

"Pinkish red."

"Oh, very good, sir. Sounds like it's strawberry. Wouldn't have done so well with lime, now would we? But strawberry, I think we can work with that. Allow me to consult the checklist, and I'll see what I can help you with."

Bronson wondered at this. He wanted to ask, aren't we in the computer age? But he thought better of it for the sake of expediency. He was in England, after all, not the USA. He did not yet completely understand their foreign ways.

"Ah, first let me ask you, sir, did you by any chance take the sharks out, sell them off, drain the tank, and then fill it up with jelly?"

Bronson thought hard. "No, no. I would most certainly remember a thing like that."

"Quite right, sir. One does tend to remember. But, just to be safe, I thought I'd start with the first item on the checklist. Now, moving along, have you hired a person to assist in the care of your tank?"

"I've got a guy. Abdel. He does a very good job."

"Now, might this Abdel have taken the sharks out, sold them off, drained the tank, and then filled it with jelly?"

"Well, I highly doubt it. But, I'll ask him." Bronson walked over to the far wall, leaned over again at an awkward angle, and opened a small cabinet perhaps three feet in height. A short, dark man was crouched inside, motionless but open-eyed. "Abdel? Are you awake?" The man popped up, startled, banging his head on the top of the cupboard. He was apparently trying to stand before realizing he was in his sleeping room. Bronson winced. "Ouch, you okay there?"

Abdel rubbed his head and spoke in his Pakistani accent, "Yes sir, I am very fine indeed. Do you require assistance tonight? I am always glad to please."

"Abdel, you didn't happen to do anything special to the sharks today, did you?"

"Oh, no, Mr. Bronson. Today is my day off. I spent the whole day in my room."

"What about yesterday?"

"No, nothing special, Mr. Bronson. They swam around. I tested the water. I fed them only one orphan as per your instructions. Is there something that does not meet with your complete satisfaction, sir?"

"Yes. Now my sharks are gone, and there is gelatin in the tank."

"Gelatin? That is indeed alarming! Most upsetting! How much gelatin?"

"Filled to the brim, Abdel. I am not pleased."

"I can assure you that I had nothing to do with this! Woe is me! Poor Leeko and Kona! Oh, Allah!"

Bronson shut the door, muffling the cries of the servant inside. He returned to his call. "No, he had nothing to do with this."

"Says so, does he, sir?"

With a slight tone of annoyance, Bronson said, "I have absolute faith in Abdel."

"Yes, it never is numbers one or two on the list. Still, we have to be thorough, sir. It just wouldn't do to miss an obvious one. We wouldn't want that snake to bite us in the proverbial arse, now would we? Now, moving along, have you recently made enemies of your neighbors, done something they might want to get revenge for perhaps?"

"I don't know. I'm at work most of the time. I don't spend much time in my flat, so... I'll go with a cautious 'no,' but don't quote me on that."

"No quotes, indeed, sir. We'll rule the neighbors out. Frankly, I'll let you in on a little secret. This sort of thing happens a lot with the SRGST 5000, though we hate to admit it. Not the first time the sharks have gone missing, and jelly turns up in their place. Just an engineering error, I believe."

"So, now what do I do?"

"First thing's first, we simply must get all that jelly out of the tank. No use in leaving it in, is there? Best way to do it: throw something of a soiree."

"A party?"

"Gala event, sir. Invite all your friends, especially those with a particular fondness for the eating of jelly. Serve a dish to every guest, and you'll be that much closer to a resolution."

"Is it going to be safe to eat? I mean to say, I'm not even sure that it is gelatin."

"We'll sort that straight away. Sending our agent over now."

Five seconds passed before Bronson's doorbell sounded. He opened the door, and a pygmy chimp capered in, wearing a cowboy hat and a t-shirt bearing a picture of President Bush. The caption read: "I'm the President, so kiss my ass." The chimpanzee looked up at Bronson, extended both middle fingers, and blew a rather loud raspberry, then hopped up and down, squealing in laughter.

"Uh... there's a chimp here in a cowboy hat."

"Yes, sorry about that. It's his night off, you see, but he was closer than any of our agents on duty. Might be a little bit cheeky, but he agreed to do the testing. So, simply stand aside and let get on with the task in hand would be my advice, sir. We'll cover any damages, of course."

The chimp ran down a short hall, thumping on the wall three times, until he came to the bedroom door, which he thumped on twice. He then turned around, shuffled on all fours back down the hall until he discovered the kitchen. After a short survey of his surroundings, he opened each drawer and cabinet, tossing everything he found onto the floor until he held one spoon and one bowl. He tottered awkwardly on just his back legs to the living room, hopped up on the tank, and spooned out a bowl of the gelatin.

"He's got a bowl of the stuff," Bronson said into his phone.

"Good. Now leave him to eat it, sir, and we'll see how he fares in a half-hour's time. In the meantime, I'll recite some Blake for you if I may. 'When my mother died I was very young, / And my father sold me while yet my tongue / Could scarcely cry "Weep! weep! weep! weep!"/ So your chimneys I sweep, and in soot I sleep....'"

Bronson eyed the ape, watching for the most infinitesimal change in demeanor or breathing pattern. Nigel continued with the poetry, although he knew Bronson wasn't paying attention. He slipped in a "What light through yonder window breaks," and Bronson didn't even chuckle. Nigel did not bother to call out the American on his ignorance. This was in keeping with the lessons of his manual "How to Speak to Rich Americans over the Phone."

After twenty-nine minutes had passed, Bronson finally interrupted Nigel: "The chimp looks fine. He's hopping around on my coffee table. He tore up one of my adult magazines. I don't think he approves of smut."

"Smashing. Of course we'll reimburse you for the torn girlie mags, sir. But good news on the soiree front, what? Have your guests eat up all that jelly, then give me a call back."

"Yeah, sure. Okay. I'll do it tomorrow night. Sounds fine. Talk to you later." After hanging up, Bronson realized the chimp was still in the apartment. "Hey, you. Don't you think it's time to go?"

The chimp said nothing but cowered from Bronson's stern tone. He hung his head, picked his cowboy hat up off the floor, and left. It almost broke the rich man's heart to see the poor creature in such a dejected state. "I'll have to remember to invite him to the party."

———◦———

The party was going nicely, but Bronson did overhear a particularly well-dressed socialite say to her friend, "I thought this fellow was rich. I don't even see any sharks." They muffled their laughter as he passed them, face a little red, suit a little rumpled. He hadn't been able to sleep the night before. Something about all that gelatin just made him uneasy. The guests seemed to be enjoying it, though. They treated it like a cute, themed affair: Jelly Night. Before too long, the entire tank had been emptied, save the usual scum that settles to the bottom. Abdel would have to take care of that in the morning.

A burley, middle-aged man with a bushy moustache approached Bronson, slapped him on the back, and said, "What an absolutely terrific place you've got here. I must say, most Americans would have something gauche, say a wide screen television, to ruin the ambience. But I like your style. Though one wonders, why keep the dessert in a shark tank? If I were you, I'd get myself a few sharks for it. Here's my card." It read:

Adrian Hawthorne
Shark Importer

It also gave the address where one could find his Fabulous Lair of Sharks. "Not just sharks, mind you," Hawthorne added. "I'm the only man in town who can set you up with proper barracuda. The other lads'll give you a dogfish with glued-on glass needles for teeth. Since I know you are a man of refined tastes, I know you wouldn't settle for that rubbish. I'll get you real barracuda, no questions asked. The other lads'll ask questions, too. 'Whatcha want with them barracuders?' they'll say. Don't take any cheek. Deal with Hawthorne. I'm your man." His spiel was much like a commercial.

Bronson waited to see if a jingle would play before saying, "Thank you, Mr. Hawthorne. I'll keep you in mind."

The party progressed well into the wee hours. Bronson was antsy and aloof but couldn't bring himself to send his guests away. They all appeared to be having such a splendid time. Some had even fallen asleep on his sofa, in his recliners, or curled up in corners using their dinner jackets as pillows. Bronson followed precedent and retired for the few hours of sleep he could manage before he had to get up to go promote his latest whatever.

———⋄———

He awoke around 6:30, stumbled out of bed and into his living room where the sleeping partygoers had all been replaced, or, rather, transformed. Large cocoons littered his rooms, smeared with gooey webs that linked them inextricably to his furniture and carpeting. "Oh, hell. What next?"

He dialed the assistance number again. *Ring, ring.* "Hello, this is Nigel speaking. How can I be of assistance today?"

"My guests have all formed cocoons."

"Ah, that's a good sign. But tell me this, did you flood your flat as soon as they fell asleep, sir?"

"Of course not. Why would I do a thing like that?"

"Tisk tisk, sir. Really should have called me back like I instructed. If you had called me after they ate the jelly, I would have told you the next item on the list would be to allow them to fall asleep, then flood your flat with salt water. Won't be much good to you now as I expect they're already dead."

Bronson's heart palpitated. His palms sweated. He went to his kitchen to retrieve a very sharp Japanese steak knife and then returned to cut one of the cocoons. He peeled back the scaly husk and revealed a slimy shark in an ill-fitting tuxedo, eyes staring abnormally blankly at him, even for shark eyes. "Dead," he confirmed. "This is great. An apartment full of dead sharks."

"We'll get this settled straight away," Nigel said.

Perhaps eight seconds passed before the doorbell sounded. It was the chimp again, this time in a blue jumpsuit, accompanied by several colleagues.

Bronson shrugged. "I'm sorry I forgot to invite you to the party. But from the looks of it, that mistake worked out for the best."

The chimp gave a dismissive wave. He and the other chimps scampered off to ransack the kitchen. They returned, each with a steak knife and fork in hand, teeth bared. Bronson began to worry harder.

"Yes," Nigel said, "we'll have this sorted in no time."

GOVERNOR OF THE HOMELESS

1

On a street corner, Wilson found the Governor of the Homeless panhandling. The man's attire did not give him away. In fact, he denied that he held any office whatsoever. He appeared to be the same as any other bum. But it had to be the Governor; Wilson believed he had a knack for knowing these things.

Wilson waited, and the city sky smeared from clear blue to simple gray to hazy brown born of the contamination of streetlights. He watched his quarry all the while, until such time as the Governor took his small dog, Beyonce, in hand and put his collection of garbage in an old shopping cart, and then moved from his corner into an alleyway that no one but cats and vagrants traversed.

Wilson buttoned his trench coat, pulled up his collar for courage, and became the Governor's shadow. He felt his snub-nose in his pocket. He lumbered taller than his five feet, four inches should have allowed. He wore dark glasses despite the lack of sun. He had shaved his head but not his face earlier in the day. The stubble, the coat, the shades, the black porkpie hat: he was a specter. The Governor didn't know what was coming for him. When we asked him about it later, Wilson insisted he had transformed during the incident. He looked at the security camera pictures and could not identify himself, unlike half a dozen eyewitnesses. His detailed recollections had some glaring gaps.

The first thing Wilson saw in the alley, according to later testimony, was the facedown body of a naked female he referred to as "The Angel." Her feathers had been plucked, but he could see her embarrassed chicken wings, curled up as if to avoid detection. He examined them and made a quick note on his pad about the scaly texture. This was introduced later as Exhibit G. The judge almost laughed when the defense team presented this in open court. I was certainly shocked and didn't know what to make of it at the time.

After he left The Angel, Wilson moved further into the alley, which became a labyrinth full of shanties and false walls that obscured God knows what. If he'd had more time, he would have busted them down and exposed their inhabitants or the troves of arcane relics they concealed. At the torn corner of a sheet hiding an opening into a disused tenement, he observed a pile of hands: all left hands of wizards, he later claimed. He was torn apart on cross-examination because there was no way he could confirm that they were all left hands.

Wilson pushed on, for he still sought the Governor who was nearly out of sight, escaping into foreboding shadows. He was able to gain a small amount of ground before he noticed the screaming. It was not, he said, the screaming of mortals. No one in the courtroom was at all surprised by that remark, not even the more skittish members of the jury who shuddered every time the prosecutor ruffled his wig. Wilson went on, saying that the scream was female, ghostly, an omen of ill fate. I wonder now why he did not heed that omen. His actions afterward seem almost childishly reckless upon reflection.

It was evident to me that Wilson was insane, and this was hardly surprising given the composition of Bum Town: the mad, the forgotten, the unclean. I cannot fault him for losing his grip on reality, for what is reality if not a consistent adherence to rules? Rules do not apply in Bum Town. Sane truth must be observed by a conforming society. Bum Town is anything but. Ask me, next time you see me, how I came to Bum Town, and maybe I will tell you a long, meandering tale that may not have anything to do with sane truth. I can only offer you my word that what I say really happened somewhere, at some time, to someone who used to be or who would become me.

But I think I was talking about Wilson.

The first time I met Wilson, I was pretending to be a lookout for a dice game. Not craps, no one has any taste for that game anymore. It was something that Chinese Charlie had devised, something similar to Mah-Jong. The numbers all represented flowers and Oriental mystical symbols. Box cars won you an egg roll if Chinese Charlie had one on him. Wilson was pretending he was interested in getting a place in the game, but I already knew he was trying to sniff out information. He couldn't wait to start asking questions about the Governor. Our first conversation went something like this:

Wilson: Hey, hey. You running this game?

Me: No way. Charlie runs these games. Chinese Charlie.

Wilson: He doesn't look Chinese.

Me: He's probably not. And I doubt his name is really Charlie.

Wilson: Charles, then, most likely.

Me: Not even. It's something with an A.

Wilson: Charles does have an A.

Me: Are you in or are you out?

Wilson: (Handing me a five) I am in. Oh, hey, buddy. Do you know anything about who runs Bum Town?

From there, he proceeded to not-so-subtly schmooze with all the other players, tossing out some of his theories about the Governor and opinions on his policies about the future security of Bum Town and the use of a nonhuman police force. His eyes were not clear, not sharp with the look of a man bent on murder. I don't know if he had convinced himself at that point that the Governor needed to pay for Dr. Chalupnik's sins. Wilson didn't make that clear in what testimony he was able to give. But he already hated Chalupnik. I remember him saying so as he left the game. Something like, "Fuck! I'm all out of dough. Oh, well, at least I have my hatred for that shitbird Doctor C." (Doctor C., he admitted on the stand, was a nickname for Chalupnik.) Though, if I'm honest, Wilson sounded more like he was reading that crap off a script than speaking from his gut.

The lunatic Wilson was on trial for killing the Governor of the Homeless, but we all knew he hadn't. The Governor was alive and sitting in the courtroom. Only Wilson believed he had killed the Governor. This trial was about something else entirely. I'm writing this to see if I can figure out what that was.

2

There was another time Wilson came around sniffing at the dice game, a lot later. It was drizzling that night, little bullseyes in the reflections of a neon sign on the cracked sidewalk. Wilson tromped right through that puddle like he didn't give a shit about having wet feet. And he was as subtle as last time:

Wilson: Hey, friend. I can't stay away. Got money to lose. Burning a hole in my pocket.

Me: Well, walk through a deeper puddle, and that fire will go right out.

Wilson: I didn't know you were funny.

Me: I don't feel funny. I feel wet. You in?

Wilson: (Handing me a five) Yeah, friend, of course. So Charlie ain't Chinese, is he?

Me: You're like a broken record. He ain't Chinese, no. I don't think so.

Wilson: What is he then?

Me: Shit, Black and Vietnamese, I think.

Wilson: No shit?

Me: I don't know. He's the boss. He runs the game. Why do you care?

Wilson: Just curious, friend.

Me: Why don't you ask him? Charlie.

Charlie comes over.

Me: This boot-nugget wants to know your freaking ancestry.

Charlie: Why? Am I inheriting money? Tell me I got a rich uncle that died with no direct heirs, and you'll make me one happy motherfucker.

Me: Nah, he wants to know your race.

Charlie: (Stares at Wilson) That right? You a racist, man?

Wilson: No. No way. (Averting his eyes.)

Charlie: Coon, Spic, and Chink with a little Kraut and Mick way back in the woodpile. Got a problem with that?

Wilson looked scared for a minute. Then he laughed nervously. Charlie patted him on the back, waved him in, and they went to play the game.

That was a weird night, if I'm recalling the correct night, because that's the night that a couple of Arboghasts showed up. Their gasmasks tight on their faces, they spoke in the clipped, mechanical tones that we all were familiar with but could never understand. They wore that red leather, dyed in blood some said, so tight and all over, which gave rise to the rumors that they were, in fact, made of leather, hollow on the inside or some gears or baby organs preserved in the amnion of a woman carrying a demon-seed. They had one of those clockwork vultures with them on a long chain. Its skeletal face stared at me, but I couldn't be sure whether it was seeing me, with the severe lack of eyes in the orbits.

At first I assumed the Arboghasts would break up the game, some new ruling from the Governor's Office. But they sort of watched the fellows play and whisper-clicked asides to one another while they fed dead snakes to their pet. It made everybody pretty nervous to have them hanging around, and you could hardly blame the rowdies playing that night, because you usually didn't see any Arboghasts unless they were out breaking heads and taking ears and fingers and foreskins as trophies.

Wilson broke off rather quickly when the game started to wind down, and the Arboghasts took note, though they didn't pursue. It could have been they put one of their tracking slugs on him to catch up to him later.

And then the mekanik carrion bird started making this horrible squawking that filled all our souls with visions of large, dingy bodies of water full of leviathans ready to rise up and eat us like we were grapes wearing dirty clothes. The rest of the boys shuffled off and Charlie glared at those two Arboghasts.

One chirped to the other, and they busted out in their stale, cardboard version of laughter, finally drifting back into the night to wherever those things go.

I said to Charlie:

Me: You see them 'ghasts, huh?

Charlie: Course I saw them. Whatchoo think, I'm blind? They fucked up the game tonight. Taking the piss out of my wind.

Me: I think they were here for the weirdo. The one who was asking about you and the Governor.

Charlie: Man, I don't know nothing about nothing. They could have just been out for some fun. Arboghasts might like fun, right? No reason why they couldn't.

Me: If they wanted fun, they'd have joined in the game.

Charlie: Maybe nervous. Never actually played before. Don't wanna make fools of theyselfs so they was just observing.

Me: Maybe.

Charlie: Man, as long as they wasn't clubbing in the heads of the players, that's good enough for me. I guess I'm going home, to bed.

That was the last time I saw Charlie in human form.

Amongst Wilson's possessions, when the Securitate tossed his room in the flophouse, was a dime-store paperback called *Abortionstein*. The book is the story of a female detective on the trail of a sadistic murderer who has been dumping the corpses of prostitutes with aborted fetuses sewn into their wombs.

Meanwhile, small, deformed children have been showing up around town, on playgrounds, etc., attacking pets and regular children. One feature ties them together: they all have cat eyes. An ancient Shawnee legend says that children with cat eyes are soulless abominations. Somehow, for no explained reason, the DNA of one of these creatures is tested and tied to a woman in town who confesses to having had an abortion in the recent past. She had been raped. An ancient Iroquois legend says that rape babies are soulless.

It becomes clear to the detective that this is the work of a madman obsessed with "reversing" the abortion procedure. He is sewing the dead fetal tissue back into the womb in hopes of breathing life back into it. Instead, the whores he has kidnapped become incredibly sick and die. But for some reason, rape babies are being "carried to term"—being revived as monsters. He wants to create healthy, normal, non-rape babies. The man is maddened by this failure.

The reverse abortions also garner the attention of a tel-evangelist in the area on a Pro-Life crusade. The evangelist mistakes the handiwork of this butcher as an attempt to fulfill the will of God, so he hires a private investigator to track the man down. Once he has discovered the doctor's lair, the evangelist sneaks in to marvel at the wonders that God has wrought by the hands of this man the media has dubbed Abortionstein. He finds a cage full of the cat-eyed children, and he releases them, thinking they are miracles. They tear the man to pieces and drink his blood.

The detective follows the evangelist and falls right into Abortionstein's trap. Dr. Chalpuniak, the man dubbed Abor-tionstein, blames his failures on the dirty wombs of the prostitutes he used as his initial subjects. He needs a clean womb, the womb of the detective, a chaste woman who has never known a man, or at least this is what Chalpuniak believes.

A wealthy eccentric who enjoys dining on fetuses ransacks Abortionstein's lair. Luckily for the detective, he stumbles upon her tied up to a table while Abortionstein is in another room. He frees her, and they rig up some dynamite and blow up the lair. We are supposed to assume Abortionstein is killed in the explosion, but then at the very end, his hand pokes out of the rubble, with bits of aborted baby stitched in with his normal flesh, suggesting a sequel.

There was no such sequel. But there was a brief listing of other works available by the author, including *Chalupacabra*, *Atomic Dinosaur Manchild*, and *One Light Year and 50 Million Kill-o-Watt Hours from Earth*. These books were not found among Wilson's possessions.

4

When Wilson was cross-examined on the stand, which consisted of little more than some old orange crates, he said he had initially been hired by Dr. Chalupnik six years ago. At first he did not understand the true nature of the man's work, but it quickly became apparent that Dr. C was not your run of the mill witchdoctor. He had some kind of laboratory hooked up, full of Tesla coils, theremins, and Van de Graaff generators. "That wasn't stuff you used for herbalism, not even in this modern age of technology," Wilson claimed.

The prosecutor, scratching the mop head he wore as a wig, asked if Dr. Chalupnik ever told Wilson he was an herbalist, and Wilson said he had not. He claimed to have never asked the man what kind of work he did or what the devices were for. This made no sense, and the prosecutor could barely contain his laughter when he asked Wilson, "How can you take a job where you don't know what's going on?" And everyone in the room burst out laughing.

Wilson said, barely loud enough to hear, "Ask anyone in government." But the remark was stricken from the record.

I think it was obvious at this point to everyone in that squalid, cellar-chamber courtroom that Wilson was a certifiable head case, but who in Bum Town was not? I started working on an old connect-the-dots I'd found in an abandoned stroller. I can't be sure if what I heard next was something I imagined or not. I seem to recall that Wilson screamed, not the scream of a grown man, but the gurgling cry of a newborn infant. It got louder and louder, but I was intent on working on the puzzle because these dots were pretty hard to connect. The judge ordered an au pair, or at least a girl who did not speak a lot of English, to tend to Wilson, to get him back in sorts so the questioning could continue. A kid in the gallery had an old pink Walkman hooked to chintzy little computer speakers, and she was playing a garbled version of "Lovely Day" by Bill Withers. The judge ordered her to turn it up and claimed this was his "jam." A few drifters in the back danced while a hag in front of me got out of her seat to vomit into one of the buckets placed in the cobwebbed corners.

A calm descended over the rabble gathered in the dank gallery, and people retook their seats upon old church pews salvaged from a burnt chapel. Wilson stopped screaming at some point and had already resumed responding normally, or as close to normal as could be expected from a nuthatch like that. He was now detailing his problem with the Street Cleaners, who, he claimed, were eating our brethren in the City proper if they should be caught out after curfew. In his mind, the Cleaners were specially bred cannibalistic mutants who dined on the street trash, living and dead. The city kept them locked up in the daylight, far from the prying eyes of the decent citizenry.

Could he have been correct? I had no idea. We all knew that bums weren't safe outside Bum Town, and given that we had something as heinous as Arboghasts prowling our streets, it seemed plausible that the City could have monstrous Street Cleaners out and about after the sun goes down.

The judge ordered him to move on. This testimony had nothing to do with the question asked. The Street Cleaners were in no way tied to either Dr. C. or the Governor, and so the thin, white-haired "child" was released from within the judge's robe. It scurried up to the stand and began whacking Wilson on his legs and arms with a rattan baton.

The defense objected to the flogging.

The judge agreed to put a nickel into the Injustice Jar, an old plastic mayonnaise container into which he chucked a coin whenever he violated due process. The jar was looking quite full, and it had been empty when the court took session that morning.

Wilson requested a consult with his sponsor.

The court was briefly adjourned.

I went outside for a smoke and a stroll.

I saw Filthy Grey Hawkins out there in a shopping cart-littered street. He had two strings on his rectangular-body guitar. "I invented this here guitar," he always claimed. "Bo Diddley done stole it up!" Filthy was only about three decades younger than Diddley, though he looked every bit of a hundred years old. His gnarled fingers glided over the guitar frets sublimely, and he could play any variety of blues or ragtime you might want to hear, or not want to hear if your tastes were more like mine.

Me: Why'ontcha give that thing a rest, Filthy?

Filthy: I let it rest, I might as well just curl up in a ball and die. My soul is the sound coming out this guitar rye-chere. Thoe me one them empty bottles for a slide.

Me: I don't know how you make any kind of sensible songs on there without the strings.

Filthy: Two is more than enough. I do more on these two than that hack Hendrix did on six. And I ain't gotta cheat and play all left-handed.

I gave him the bottle, and he made those dual wires buzz with a song that could make a certain type of person cry. But I am not that type of person. I don't care for the blues.

A yappy stray dog came up to us, barking especially at Filthy. I told it to shush. Filthy kept on playing, acting like the dog was singing along with him. I was about to run the noisy beast off when I saw the shadowy form of something buzzard-like ooze from the sky down onto the little barking thing. It grabbed the dog's hind quarters in its talons and decapitated the mutt with its metal beak. The vultures usually don't sic live quarry without a command from their Arboghast handlers. I thought maybe it smelled the stink coming off Filthy and mistook it for the odor of carrion.

Me: That wasn't your dog, was it?

Filthy: No. No, man. But it ain't deserve to go out like that. That ain't right!

Me: Yeah, bothers me that I don't see this bird's keeper anywhere around.

Filthy: Can they get free? Turn all feral?

Me: I guess that's possible. Happens a lot in old sci-fi movies.

Filthy: It's a lot scurrier in real life.

Me: Yeah.

Then the thing flew away with what little remained of the dog in its grip.

5

Somehow I was able to get ahold of evidence from the case. A few dozen pages of a typewritten manuscript for something called *Clean Streets*, presumably written by Wilson. It read like a pulp novel, though it was supposedly a historical novel based on rigorous research of the present era. This seemed to imply that he thought everything he had made up on the page was a reflection of reality.

It was clear at this point that Wilson's thinking was de-ranged. Somehow he'd become convinced there were large

flesh-eating monsters loose in the City to purge it of unde-
sirables—that this was a plan put into action by some mu-
nicipal committee for the improvement of the community. It
was farfetched, but there was something compelling in the
earnestness of the prose that troubled me more so than the
fact Wilson had put a slug in the back of some poor bastard's
head thinking he was the Governor. It's one thing to kill a man;
it's quite another to concoct some kind of reality on the page
that deliberately twists and perverts a man's mind.

The story followed a cast of sympathetic characters, including the obligatory shot-gun-wielding man of action, a
mentally impaired maiden fair, two young boys with filthy
striped shirts, one of the handlers of the Street Cleaners
themselves who was quite conflicted about her job, and a
corrupt cop who winds up killing everybody at the end. (The
last two pages of the story were included with the others.)

A few of the passages return to me every once in a while.
They've pushed out my own private daydreams with this
half-dystopian, half-romanticized doom. Sometimes I see a
kid staggering along some side street, and he's wearing a
striped shirt, and it's filthy. And I just lose it. I just break down
right there, weeping like a baby for the childhood I lost in the
fire.

They burned my fucking brain. Not a lot of people can say
that.

6

One time Wilson brought his girlfriend to the dice game.
She was missing an arm but was otherwise pretty attractive
in an alley-cat sort of way. Red hair, the color of spray paint.
Smokey eyes from the fact she never removed her makeup.
She'd led a hard life—you could see that. But you could also
see she knew how to have a good time, which made it puzzling
why she'd be with Wilson, who was the place you go to stare
into the internal void of tedious existence. He was a stick

in the mud, a wet blanket, a killjoy, a party pooper, and a spoilsport. Sometimes all at once.

As the game progressed, this girl wandered off into alcoves with a couple different guys under the pretext that they were going to smoke. Everyone shooting dice was already smoking, so I figured she must be hooking. A handy or a blowjay for some of the fellas to put a little bit of coin in Wilson's pocket to waste on the game.

Later, when I talked with the guys she'd gone off with, they said she was giving it away for free, but she kept asking a bunch of questions about the Governor and Bum Town, asking if they knew Chalupnik or anything about the Street Cleaners.

So Wilson must've hired her to try to get tongues wagging by getting cocks throbbing. None of the guys had any useful information though, and most had at least gonorrhea.

Meanwhile, Wilson was standing by, betting just enough to make it look as if he were interested in the game.

"You know people used to be able to fly in the prehistoric times," he said out of nowhere while the girl was off reconnoitering.

"That's bullshit," Charlie said. A bunch of the others laughed. We didn't know what he was talking about.

"It's true. People now only use about ten percent of their brain. In those days, they used pretty much the whole thing. And they could fly."

I thought he meant psychic powers, but he went on: "They used their huge brains—because they had those big foreheads, so their brains were bigger—they used those brains to figure out how to saddle up pteranodons and fly those buggers around the sky."

Kep, the old cardsharp, squinted, bared his four teeth and asked, "What the fuck a terranondon?"

Wilson, very seriously, elucidated: "The media commonly refer to all flying reptiles of the dinosaur era—and they are not dinosaurs—as pterodactyls. But those are only one specific type of pterosaur, like their distant cousins the pteranodons."

"So, flying dinosaurs?" asked Rip Ravel, a legally blind ex-trucker.

"Well, they are not technically dinosaurs, but the media call them that."

"So, what is they?" Kep said. "Dragons?"

Wilson's eyes went narrow, in rage or disgust. I couldn't tell. "If you can't figure out what I'm talking about, I'm done here," he said, and went quiet.

And I looked up into the grimy night sky there, and in the moonlight, I could sort of make out the silhouette of a giant bird. Was it a bird? Was it an Arboghast on some clockwork vulture big enough to ride? Was it a genius caveman on a pterodactyl?

Was it a dragon?

Theory I heard was that dinosaurs never actually died out. They simply evolved over time into other things, basilisks and wyverns. Or maybe just birds. But here's the interesting thing: when I was in school, they showed us all these pictures of this thing called Archaeopteryx. Sort of a lizard with feathery wings. Now, they told us that it couldn't actually fly, but it could glide. How they knew this, I'm not sure. Not like they had the Zapruder footage of Wilbur and Orville Archaeopteryx trying to get off the ground. And they said that, over time, this monster gave birth to another monster that was slightly more like a bird until, eventually, they actually could fly. And then all birds came out of that, even those that don't fly. They lost that gift somewhere down the line.

Years later, I saw a book that said Archaeopteryx was an evolutionary dead end, but he had a cousin who was similar, and the cousin was the one who fathered all of birdkind. But the thing is: this cousin was only theorized to exist. They didn't actually have the fossils to prove it, but he had to exist because their theory was sound. It couldn't have happened any other way. They wouldn't have come up with this model if it wasn't the best one.

Archaeopteryx, in case you are getting any zany thoughts, was way too small to ride, even if it could fly. You might be able to tape a gerbil to its back, just for the sake of science.

Kep laughed at Wilson, drawing me out of my reverie. Wilson was more or less pouting. "This fool think he's a prophet of science or some shit."

"Now that you mention it," Wilson said, "I do have a prediction about the future of science." He seemed to be re-engaged, enthusiastic again.

"Oh, yeah, professor?" joked Chinese Charlie. "Why don't you remove the blinkers of ignorance from our fucking eyes"—he pretended to pull away a blindfold and see for the first time—"and enlighten us?"

Wilson looked like he didn't even hear the mocking tone in the men's voices. He puffed himself up a bit, ready to impart some really valuable bit of wisdom to younger siblings. Or like he was about to tell a scary story around the campfire.

"You know how technology has gotten smaller? In the Fifties, computers used to take up an entire room. By the Eighties, a computer could fit on your desktop and had more power than all those reel to reel monsters you see in the old movies. In the Seventies, calculators sat on your desk. By the Eighties, they could fit in your pocket. The trend is for technology to get smaller and smaller. Now people have computers they refer to as phones that have more power than all the computers that existed in the Eighties put together."

Kep nodded, looking surprised. "Yep. That's true. What comes next?"

"In the future," Wilson continued, "maybe sixty years from now, maybe eighty, things will get so small that people can no longer use them. It's the singularity that many have predicted. Total power in our technology, but far more minuscule than any human can make use of. So we return to the Dark Ages as barbarians, barely able to remember what pencils are for."

"Fuck, you talkin' Mad Max? Road Warrior?" Rip Ravel asked with a raucous snort.

"Oh, shit! I'm all about some post-apocalyptic barbarian action!" Charlie said, giving high fives to Kep and Rip, but Wilson left him hanging.

"It's not going to be a fun time, gents. It's going to be the end," Wilson said.

The end. Like Archaeopteryx, I wondered? We die while our weird cousins go on to evolve small enough to operate the teeny-tiny gizmos the future holds. Freaking gremlins inside the gears and mechanisms or, what do they have now, diodes and capacitors? Small enough to wander around inside the fiber optic cables. Small enough to inhabit the empty spaces between electrons and nuclei. Really fucking itty-bitty. Possibly giving new meaning to 'quantum mechanics.' They could be in there, in the future, tinkering with the positions of sub-atomic particles with minute wrenches they pull from their teensy tool belts.

Or maybe Wilson is a lunatic who doesn't know what he's talking about. Still, if he's led me to a dead-end, there's got to be some way of getting to point B from point A. You can always get there from here.

7

When younger guys, still green behind the ears, who look up to me ask me if I've seen much action, I have a favorite story I always enjoy telling. I tell them, one night I was out on the streets, not in a capacity as an enforcer—I had the night off. But I was packing a Desert Eagle tucked into my waistband.

Two Arboghasts rolled up the street. Both in tight, shiny, brand-new-looking red leather. They were outfitted with some new gadgetry that I'd never even seen before. I knew they had to be there hunting. The slightly taller one gurgled loudly and pointed down to the far end of the street.

I turned to look and saw only another Arboghast. This one was thicker, like he'd been packed full of loose sausage almost to the point of bursting his darker, stained leathers. He was covered in long spikes, not the studs you see on young kids who want to play at being tough or goth or whathaveyou. These things were as sharp as pitchfork tines and almost as long. He was a throbbing porcupine stuck inside a slick jumpsuit. Holes in his false skin showed the metal-rod *bones* that truly composed these automata. He lurched forward at an alarming rate. I had no idea what was going on.

It was mere seconds before this larger Arboghast was upon the two smaller, newer models. The rending and shredding commenced, and though the big guy's condition made him more vulnerable, he moved with such deadly cunning that the other two could not gain a sufficient grip upon him to work free his boney infrastructure.

He ripped them, colloquially, new assholes—all over their bodies. He pulled out metal rods and things that looked as if they were once alive, all of which he discarded as so much rubbish on the street there and in the gutters.

What could it mean? Warring factions? A struggle for who would control Bum Town?

The big one snapped the final brittle remnants of the others and scattered bits of the carcasses with the fervor of a cage-raised fighting dog. And then he came right up to me.

He looked at me with his dead eyes. I saw my pitiful, shocked reflection in the black glass of his welder's goggles. I didn't shit my pants, and I wondered at the moment how anyone could shit themselves in this kind of situation. I had the opposite reaction: a clenching of all my body's sphincters. I couldn't have relieved myself if I'd tried. I'm shit-shy, I guess. But even without soiling myself, I knew terror in that moment. The embodiment of death and judgment and insanity right there glaring at me.

But—and this is the part that really impresses most people—I reached out my bare hand and I swatted him on the muzzle.

He jerked his head side to side in confusion, letting out a squeal that released a reddish smoke from a narrow slit in his tree-trunk of a neck. Verminous things leaked from his snapping maw. It bounced back from me like an ape, sizing me up.

And then he huffed and turned and stalked off.

That's one version of the story. Truthfully, I can't remember which version is correct, but I don't think it matters.

The other version sounds awfully similar to a passage from a book that I'm pretty sure I didn't write, causing me to wonder how it snuck into my life.

In this version, I'm at the very edge of Bum Town where it meets the old City. The two young Arboghasts are guarding Bum Town, I think. And a Street Cleaner charges them—somehow, the invisible fence has failed, and he's loose. I should be panicking, but I'm just standing there, watching the fight. He's a head and half taller than either of those 'ghasts. He's nothing I've ever seen. He's got a prehensile tail that he uses to pull off one of their heads. It pops like a cork from a bottle of champagne, and the thing's vital essence sluices out like molasses full of cigarette butts and maggots.

He's just doing his job. I can't blame him. If the Arboghasts are anything, they are filth. And they need to be cleaned.

Anyway, there's another possible version of this story, which is that it didn't ever happen at all. It's the least impressive variation, so I generally do not put this one forward first. If I did, I would sound the same as Brownhouse Petey. He used to say stuff like, "One time nothing happened." He was a lunatic. Now he's dead. Now nothing happens to him all the time.

8

Wilson's trial reconvened. He was led back into the courtroom, head now shaved, hands bound with hog wire. The words *slave* and *garbage* had been carved with a razor into his arms. He wore a look of bemusement on his face, like a guy who recently got a heavy dose of toxic shock treatment. It appeared they had taught him a lesson that stuck.

"Can you tell us your name?" asked the prosecutor.

"Yes," Wilson said, staring down at his feet.

The prosecutor laughed, and the defense attorney joined him.

"Okay, Mr. Wilson...where were we?" the prosecutor said, putting his finger to his chin and staring at the ceiling histrionically.

"In an old boiler room that had been converted to a torture chamber," Wilson answered flatly.

"Good Lord, man! I didn't mean a literal location! I'm talking about where I left off with the questioning."

"You were asking me about Chalupnik."

"Yes, yes, I was. *Good doggie!*" He reached out to scratch Wilson's bald head.

The courtroom erupted in catcalls, guffaws, and jeering.

The judge quieted the court by hammering a finishing nail into the pile of debris that passed as his bench.

"That's enough of that for now. Save some for later when his goose is really cooked."

"Where," asked the pacing lawyer, "did you first meet Dr. Chalupnik?"

Wilson looked at the judge and then at the jury.

"I... It was at a party. A soiree at the Governor's mansion."

"Do you expect us to believe that a dignitary such as the Governor would allow a piece of garbage like you into the midst of his echelon?"

"I was incognito."

"So you went there under false pretenses?"

"At the time," Wilson said lucidly, "I was just another loyal admirer of what I saw as a great man, a visionary, a leader. I had no idea what he was capable of at that point."

"So you went there under true pretenses?"

"I went there, pretense or no."

"And did the Governor himself introduce you to Dr. Chalupnik?"

"No, I was introduced to Dr. C. by a woman who brewed beer for the Governor."

"Did you see Dr. Chalupnik and the Governor converse at any point?"

"I don't believe so," Wilson said, grimacing. "I'm not entirely clear."

"In that case, please enlighten the court as to the connection between those two gentlemen."

Wilson coughed, trying to stall. "Dr. C. told me on at least two occasions that he was working directly under the Governor."

"So based on the word of a madman," said the prosecutor, "whom you claim to not even know what sort of work he did, you decided that the Governor was thereby responsible for the reverse-abortion experiments?"

Where was he going with this? What was the point of this line of questioning? It would seem long overdue to let the poor schmuck off the hook, tell him the Governor was not dead. The man he had killed was a nobody, and he'd only get a slap on the wrist for not seeking permission before he took him out.

I still had no idea what was going on here. Was it all playacting for Wilson's torment? This had gone way too far. Perhaps it was playacting, but for the benefit of some other audience. The gallery, the bystanders, the rest of Bum Town.

A psychodrama reinforcing how important the Governor truly was.

And it was certainly no secret that the role and efficacy of the Governor had long been in question, gossip drifting glibly from lip to lip among the denizens of this forgotten district as they gambled, groused, and glommed on to anything that brought them a slight sense of control. Knowing your place in the universe, even one as chaotic as Bum Town, was still an essential part of the man-bum psyche. I like to know where I stand and who not to stand too close to. In Bum Town, there are more reasons to keep your distance than just the stench, because everything stinks pretty equally. That's just a trick. A trick of the nose to keep you smell-blind to the real soul sharks, perched delicately on the psychic shoreline, exactly where ether meets the meat.

Somewhere outside, I heard glass smashing. I heard a squeal that could only come from one of those mechanical carrion birds. The Arboghast bailiff started clapping, encouraging the court to join him. And he slipped over and pulled down the projector screen. The room went dark, and an old movie flickered to life.

9

Black and white, or not quite—sepia tone, maybe. Filmed in the days of early talkies, or at least in that style. It's a Robin Hood movie, or something taking place in the Crusades, or sword and sorcery. I'm not sure it matters. The dialogue is stilted, sort of like a half-wit trying to sound like Shakespeare, but sounding more like Dickens, who, I'm pretty sure, never swung a sword in his life. Dickens, if he was ten and American and wrote Christmas pageants for local performance. The backdrop appears to be a castle of cardboard. Fanfare erupts, triumphant and bombastic.

There's a guy, about forty, with a bushy mustache. He's in plate armor, with a chain coif on his head. A broad sword in his hand. His coat of arms, as seen on his gamberson, depicts a horse with a lion head. There is no name for the creature in any known lore; I looked it up later. This man is, I am willing to bet, a knight.

There's a woman, about twenty-five, with long blonde hair. She's wearing a dirty peasant dress, but her hair and make-up are perfect. She's attractive after a Northern European idealist fashion. I'm willing to bet she was a name that men knew in her day; her picture tacked to the wall in the pool hall or garage. She has a tattoo of the same nameless lion-horse on her left cheek.

"Lo, it has been quite a time at the wars! Now ten years agone I left thee as but a child with her daisy chains! All anon I love thee, Shandandra. Take the finger bones of my enemies as a token of my chivalrous affections." He pulls out a sack about the size of a human head and dumps the phalanges into her lap. She bundles them up in her skirts and giggles.

"Alack, I should have deigned to deliver ruth unto the wretches, the infidels. Peradventure, I could have made friends out of them after only a sound beating about the head and chest with my mace. Alas, 'twas not to be. Soothly, I preferred to cut off the fingers and save their bones as a trophy for my future wife.

"Future wife?" says the girl, batting her eyes.

"Why yes, Shandandra. My future wife," says the knight, leaning his head toward hers, placing his hand softly upon her chin. Pressing the button that causes her face plate to detach. He rips her dress, which tears easily in half and falls away, to reveal a mechanical but highly feminine and streamlined android.

"Future wife," she says mechanically.

He feeds finger bones to her champing, robotic maw. Each time she swallows a finger, smoke billows from her ears. I'm not sure if this is intended to be slapstick comedy or something more surreal.

"Eat! Eat, my lovely," the knight says and chortles, flicking his head back spiritedly. "You are so much better than the tin men of the ancient philosophers, animated only by so much chemical marriage. You have a working jaw! Why else does a man go hither to fight battles but to bring home a doggie bag of ears, noses, and fingers to feed to his future wife?"

A man in a rubber dragon suit shambles into the shot, looks around confused. The knight turns and shakes his head, glances into the camera. The dragon man backtracks, removing himself from the frame.

Then we get to the part that is probably why they were showing us this movie in the courtroom.

A midwife, hysterical, runs up to the knight, wailing. She's clutching a baby.

"The boy was born still! The boy was born still! There's no spirit within him!"

"Calm thyself, witch!" shouts the knight. He backhands the woman across the face and takes the dead babe from her grasp. "Future wife! Prepare thy womb!"

The future wife obliges, lying on her back and spreading her legs.

The knight crouches and forces the newborn inside the mechanical vagina. He pushes the crown all the way in, and amber lights flash on the future wife's abdomen.

"What is a-happ'nin'?" the old midwife says, doddering and nearly swooning.

"The child is being returned to life. The future wife has a pure womb, a safe haven to incubate him further, rendering him whole. In time, he will be reborn."

"O forsooth?" the woman squeals. "Thank ye, Sir Chupalkin! The mother shall be very well pleased!"

"Mention it not! Tell no one what you have seen here! Go forth and sin no more!"

And then the film cut out, and the lights came back on in the room.

11

I had a dream recently. At first, I could not recall very much of its content. But it so happens that something triggered me to remember the entire thing in almost crystalline detail.

It started, or I became aware of the dream at first, in a mansion. Not opulent, not a mansion by any sane world standards. It was, in fact, an old factory warehouse that had been crudely renovated and filled with all manner of odd *objets d'art*. Most of these masterpieces were salvaged junk: Oscar the Grouch-style trashcans forming elephant legs, pieces of car engines composing a startling simulation of a hi-fi, old pipe and wire bundled into the hair of pretty garbage ladies. There were about a dozen servants, each outfitted with Halloween-costume-shop-versions of their traditional attire. The maids wore skimpy, polyester skirts, wielding long unusable feather dusters. The butlers appeared to be extras from a Hammer horror film. And there was a brewer – a comically grotesque woman in her fifties dressed as a serving wench. But she carried herself in such a way that I knew she was in touch with the upper echelon. And it became apparent that things worked here in the opposite way. Servants were leaders. Scum was treasure. Brewers brewing not intoxication, but enlightenment. I knew that I could imbibe a beer that would make me wise if this woman would be generous enough to offer some to me.

She wryly smirked when she saw that I wanted to catch her eye. Wiggling her bulbous nose, she sidled up to me, rumpled bosom spilling out over the top of her bodice.

"I know what boys like," she said. But in my head, I knew she was not hitting on me. She was referring to that old song, but at the same time, she was letting me know that she understood what it was I sought.

From under her apron, she produced a bottle. An old-fashioned stopper on top. No label. A thick layer of tallow covering it.

I must have grimaced because she saw the hesitation and pulled the bottle back.

"Johnny, are you queer?" she said.

I shook my head, but I was still reluctant to drink the strange brew she was offering me.

The bawdy woman cracked a snaggle-toothed smile.

"Our lips are sealed." She mimicked turning a key on her closed mouth and tossed it away.

Me: When I drink that, what's going to happen to me?

Brewer: How should I know? You are your own man, aren't you?

Me: I guess so. Sure. But what happens to others?

Brewer: None of my business.

Me: Aren't you curious?

Brewer: Not in the slightest. I don't have time for worrying about the aftershocks of Truth.

Me: Does anyone ever die from drinking your beer?

Brewer: Sometimes.

Me: They *die*?

Brewer: Shhh. Voices carry.

Me: Well, I don't want to die.

Brewer: I don't think you have much choice in the matter, darling.

Me: I want to know the truth.

Brewer: Then drink this. (Handing me the bottle.)

Me: (Accepting it but looking it over carefully.) Where is it brewed?

Brewer: (Shrugging.) Hong Kong Garden.

Me: Chinese beer? Is it really Chinese?

Brewer: It's probably not. I doubt its name is really Charlie.

Me: Charles then... do beers have names? I mean, first names—personal names, in the way people have names.

Brewer: I don't know. I don't think it matters. Would you drink a Willy or a Sam?

Me: As long as it's not a swill, I'll be happy.

Brewer: Hogs drink it, but so do brain scientists.

Me: Like water.

Brewer: More like *uisce beatha. Aqua vitae. Eau de vie.*

Me: So, there are immortal pigs running around.

Brewer: No, there are drunk pigs running around. Now drink the damn thing and join them.

I drank the damn thing, pulling the stopper and guzzling it as quickly as I was able. I didn't taste anything at the time, but later, when I thought of it, it tasted like stale copper pipe kept in a cupboard at your grandmother's house behind an expired skull of some family pet that died before your conception. It's funny how in dreams, you get not only the impression of something, but an impression of that impression, and you can dream the past at the same time, or even after, the present. I didn't taste it in the past, yet I knew what it tasted like in the future. That's crazy shit once you think about it.

In the right-center area of my brain, the potion deposited a parasite that formed a cyst of knowledge that grew so large so fast my mind popped like an overfilled balloon. And it was then that I could see it: this brewer was no brewer. The Governor was no governor. And whoever was pulling the strings behind the scenes was protected by his prominent puppet.

I woke up feeling as if it were three days ago. Or I woke up way in the future, in a courtroom. Either way, I woke up, and I understood what at first I would never have believed. We had been duped. And maybe Wilson, that head case, was right.

12

In high school, they made us all read *Julius Caesar*. The textbook had more footnotes explaining to us how to read the text than there was actual story. It got pretty boring toward the end. But the main thing I think we are all supposed to get out of *Julius Caesar* is how democracy is evil, and monarchy is great. Shakespeare lived under a monarch, so he probably was scared to make the conspirators into heroes. But from a modern American high schooler's perspective, of course Brutus is the hero of the thing. He's bringing down a tyrant—a guy who had the power of a dictator and the popularity of a rock star. Even John Wilkes Booth got that much out of the story, and he was a goddamn actor, so he'd probably read Shakespeare repeatedly until it sounded natural to him instead of stuffy and pompous and half-witted.

If you lived in a country, let's say—the size of a small city—, that was ruled over by a guy who no one elected, no one could check or override, and no one even knew what he looked like, would you be a Brutus or an Antony?

Now, the thing is, the conspiracy to make Brutus out to be a blustering thug did not end with Shakespeare. It was just getting started. Take a look at *Popeye*. After he got a makeover in the Sixties, Bluto was Brutus. He was a real dick, too, constantly fucking with Popeye, who even someone in Shakespeare's time would have known to be the hero. Why change the already established Bluto's name, unless you wanted to impeach the credibility of the original Brutus, the emperor slayer? The fucking hippies were suddenly pawns of the monarchists, filling the cartoons and comics with propaganda.

And it got worse. The hippies were pushing evolution really hard. Archaeopteryx was their poster boy. They were getting that lizard-bird tattooed on their tits and sprayed on the sides of their microbuses. Two years after Darwin's masterwork sewed God's cocoon shut once and for all, they pulled that unholy fossil from the earth, seeming to prove his theories in a single stroke. But I told you before—Archaeopteryx was a dead end. It was his cousin that would have made Darwin proud. Just seeing a reptile with feathers was enough to make a Victorian-era gentleman piss in his trousers. There can't be a God if there's something like that slithering around. What kind of villain would let that happen if he had the power to stop it? This is commonly known as The Problem of Archaeopteryx.

And the hippies didn't know what hit them when that beast returned from space, gliding down by his own power from the mothership. People were calling him Quetzalcoatl. Suddenly Aztecs were taking to the streets in their headdresses and wooden armor. That's what I hated about the Sixties. It wasn't a time for sane people. You couldn't simply go about your daily routine, go to work, go to the bowling alley, go to the grave of the elders, go to the Vanishing Temple. No, not without being assaulted by flying lizards in the name of progress, freedom, and being groovy.

And what if—what if that goddamn creature was still here among us? What guise would he need to take in order to avoid being put in a glass case in some museum? The form of a man. The form of a Governor?

And where would he hide his eggs? Incubators would be a dead giveaway. He'd have to get creative. Set up a lab. Put the eggs inside prostitutes. Keep them there until they ate their way free.

It all made perfect sense. Wilson was right. Even though what Wilson had claimed on the stand bore little resemblance to this truth I had uncovered, I knew he was using a form of code to get the information across to me without arousing the suspicions of the Winged Lizard Emperor. The ersatz Governor was among us in the courtroom—why not the hidden Governor? Only one way to draw him out...

13

As I stood up, the judge was mumbling some kind of instructions to the jury, which comprised sixty-six bag ladies between the ages of sixty-five and sixty-seven, each with her stroller or trolley full of collectable rubbish. The jury had the best seats in the house: the Naugahyde bench seats from various 1970s sedans.

"Now, ladies and crones of the jury, please understand that the last demonstration was only evidence in the same way that a fossil is evidence of evolution. I think you take my meaning, but in case you don't, I've written up note cards in Sanskrit and Phoenician, and I'll have the bailiff pass them to you now."

The gangly Arboghast stagger-stagger-crawled his way to the bench. His fists flicked down upon the stack of notecards, like those of a praying mantis clutching at its delectable prey.

"Excuse me," I said softly several times as I tried not to trample the feet of those sitting in my row. Once I reached the aisle, the Arboghasts started closing in, so I didn't have much time. I walked right up to the Governor, or the man we were told was the Governor, pointed my snub-nose right in his face and yelled, "*Sic Semper Archaeopteryx!*"

I fired all six shots before the metallic talons bit into my shoulder, then my arms, driving me down to the floor. The Arboghasts clapped their crude shackles on me, making plastic clicks to one another, while in the background I could hear Wilson hooting, a mix of anxiety and happy surprise.

"He's dead! The Governor's been deaded!" cried some poor rube.

"He's not dead!" I said, face eating dirty shag carpet, tasting cat piss. "He's fucking flying around, laying eggs and shit!"

"Bailiffs!" the judge croaked. "Haul this man to the Cannery!"

Something heavy and narrow and metal hit me in the back of the skull. A blunt head trauma, I think they call it. Blackness ensued.

14

Every inhabitant of Bum Town had heard of the Cannery. It's the kind of place that everyone said you never came out of once you went in. I always figured it was malarkey. But in a matter of moments, I'd find out.

Upon coming around, the first thing I noticed was the smell of fish. The place hadn't been used in years, but the smell lingered like a pervert in the women's room, staying behind to sniff the toilet seats.

The second thing I noticed was my hands were tied. A single lamp shone down from the high ceiling, lighting the space immediately surrounding me. I was in an old wooden chair like the ones around my grandmother's dinner table. But instead of facing my grandmother eating her grits, I faced a man. He was just at the edge of the yellow light. A small man whose face I could not make out. A small man with a spectral appearance.

"Who the fuck are you?" I muttered, tongue slurring because it was only half awake.

"I might ask you the same thing," the guy said.

I told him my name. I had nothing to hide.

"Ah, that's what we thought. You've been a hard nut to crack. But even a toothless squirrel cracks a skull every once in a while." He rummaged in a green lawn and leaf bag and pulled out a portfolio. "You recognize this?"

"Huh?" I said.

"This was among the evidence in the Wilson case," he said. "I wonder if you wouldn't mind reading this." He held up a title page of a manuscript.

"*Clean Streets*," I said aloud. "By..."

"Go on, read it," the guy said, his lips curling down into a frown.

"No... that's not right."

My name on the byline.

"Yes, I'm afraid it is right."

"I'm not a writer!" I protested.

"You may not be, but you were once." He put the paper back in the portfolio, then shot his hand back into the sack and came out with a paperback, which he tossed into my lap. It was a copy of *Abortionstein*. "You wrote this one under a pseudo-name."

"I don't understand. I have no idea what's going on."

"You think Quetzalcoatl is gonna let you run around Bum Town without paying the tribute?"

He stepped into the light, let it shine upon his face. When I got a better look at him, I saw that it was Wilson.

"What the fuck is going on here, Wilson?"

"I just want to know what you know, or what you think you know, about the Governor," he said. He dropped the trash bag and pulled a pair of pliers from his pants pocket. Two more men approached. Both looked exactly like Wilson but with different hairstyles. One had a mustache. One had a scar on his cheek. But they had on the gimp suits that Arboghasts wore, which really slimmed them down. And they made that squelching sound as they moved toward me. Each one had his chosen implement of information extraction held white-knuckled in one or the other of his mitts.

They spread my legs and tilted me back. Maybe this wasn't a wooden dinner table chair. And perhaps I wasn't even in a cannery. Was it an operating room? The light was too bright in my eyes to tell.

The first Wilson undid my fly, grabbed my dick with the pliers, and pulled until I thought my brain would slide down into my gut. The screaming was unimaginable to me, so much so that my mind rejected the possibility that the noises were originating from me. They had to be torturing some other schmuck in the next room. It could not be me that was bawling.

As he yanked on my cock, one of the others took sheers and stuck one of the tips into my ass, cutting my asshole through. It felt like I was shitting glass. Fire and stabbing and scraping that would not subside. Somehow, they had taken off my pants completely without my realizing it.

The other one stabbed me in the arm with a basting needle. Hooked up an IV of some kind.

And then it happened: the first Wilson slipped back. My dick had come free. But as I watched in abject revulsion, no blood gushed forth. There was merely a hole there, where it had been attached. It was a socket, the plug-in kind you can put on hoses.

The second Wilson cut the tissue between the socket and the asshole in a few snips. And then another Arboghast approached, but it had Chinese Charlie's head sewn onto an awkwardly long, pale neck. His eyes stared toward me, yet the face showed no recognition. He held a grayish alien baby with an oblong head and dead, reptilian eyes. Its head lolled to the side, drooping like over-cooked broccoli stalks.

The first Wilson spread my legs even further, placing my feet in stirrups. I could feel two slimy hands inside.

"This won't hurt a bit," he assured me.

Truth to tell, pain does not adequately describe what I felt in that moment. But as the small being was shoved inside me and that odd feeling slid past my crotch and into my abdomen, my mind was only fixed on one amazing fact, something that would never have occurred to me that morning before I joined the gallery for Wilson's trial. One revelation that I could not deny and that brought a strange sense of accomplishment to my fragile psyche:

I was going to be a momma.

CHEMTRAIL CHAMELEON

Marlon finished reading the sixteenth issue of *Blood Soldier*, the goriest comic ever known to man—or at least to Marlon. The comic followed Sgt. Cork, a heart-broken draftee who resorted to cannibalizing his men to survive the harsh winters of Northern Germany. He and his captain, a man with no discernible facial features simply called Cap, were the sole survivors of their mission to kill the Arch-Bismarck. To Marlon's sixteen-year-old mind this was the greatest story ever told, and he could not wait for the next edition to be released.

Marlon switched off his cassette player, stopping right in the middle of the guitar solo on *Please Don't Burn My Spleen Out* by Jagged Heresy, his favorite band ever. He'd tried to cut his bangs just like the lead singer had them in 83 and had fashioned a little pentacle necklace for himself from gum wrapper foil.

He bustled downstairs to his kitchen to eat some sugary cereal crap that his mother grudgingly let him buy because she had no concept of discipline, and Marlon was a particularly willful child when it came to his breakfast options. "I'd sooner eat a bullet than an egg," he'd told her many times. "I would put a shotgun in my mouth before a sausage," was another gem of his. Once, he'd shouted, "I'll kill myself before I dine on pancakes!" That was at a Howard Johnson's. And at the IHOP, he'd declared, "Same thing applies to waffles, mom! I'll slit my own belly open like a disgraced samurai if you make me sit and eat this shit!" In other words, he was a typical teen.

As he poured himself a large bowl of Korn Smakks, the kitchen telephone rang. This was in the days when telephones were actually telephones, and they plugged into the wall. He answered the phone. It was Chemtrail Chameleon, his best friend.

"What's up, scaly dick?" Marlon joked.

"Nothing your mom can't handle, dude," Chemtrail Chameleon replied.

"I'd appreciate it if we didn't talk about my mom right now. I was just thinking about all the times she was trying to get me to eat food."

"Understood, duderino. Anyway, are we still on to see *Blood Soldier: The Movie* at eleven? Matinee rates, King Dude."

"Of course, I just gotta—"

A barrage of banging sounded from the front door of his house.

"Uh, someone's at the door. I'll see you at a quarter to 11. Bye."

"Buh-bye, dudinini."

A frumpy man of average height stood outside the front door. A ten-gallon hat topped his perfectly oval face. He wore a t-shirt with bold red lettering that spelled out "YA-HOOOOO!"

"Hi, I'm Andrew Lloyd Webber, and I'm here to tell ya sumpin' 'bout savin's!"

"Not interested," Marlon said, slamming the door as the sound of pre-recorded gunfire erupted on his doorstep. It would have been much more exciting if this were the real Andrew Lloyd Webber outside his house, bringing good tidings of great bargains, but it was just one of the many android facsimiles that Mr. Webber sent out to do his bidding, because he was a very busy man.

Chemtrail Chameleon hung up the phone. For a moment, he worried that his old man wouldn't let him go to the movies. His dad had been on another bender and never acted kindly or rationally once three sips of whiskey had passed his lips. Chemtrail Chameleon knew he would be in big trouble if his dad awoke in a stupor and he wasn't home, so he decided to wake the old man to tell him where he was headed.

He ran his scaly hand over his coarse face and tried to compose himself. Being the only CHEMTRAIL chameleon in the family always caused a sense of wrongness in him when he faced crises, even ones as small as telling his dad he was going to the movies with a friend.

The old man was splayed out on the couch like a dead pigeon.

Chemtrail Chameleon cleared his throat.

"Dad," he said weakly.

His father dozed away in whiskey-soaked oblivion.

"Dad!" he barked.

With a snort, his dad ceased snoring and opened his bleary eyes.

"What the fuck do you think you're doing? I'm in the middle of work. Don't bother me."

"You're napping on the couch in the daytime, dad."

"Don't tell *me* what I'm doing. I got a new job. I test out the best fucking napping positions on furniture for that Viking home furnishings company that just opened up in town. The one with the fag couple in their commercial."

"Uh... okay."

His father wobbled himself upright to a seated position. "Aren't you proud of your old man for getting a fancy job with a European firm?"

"Uh... sure. Congratulations."

"It's 1994, and I'm employed again! Shutting down the old gin mill was never going to stop me, you damn Japs!" He shook his fist wildly and stared at the ceiling because he believed the Japanese were spying on him from their flying saucers.

"But... the mill was torn down to build the IKEA, dad."

"Sounds like a classic ching-chong name for that maneuver, don't it?" The old man scratched his crotch and looked at his reptilian son. "You got a real sticky tongue, don't you, boy?"

"I guess?"

"Do you guess, or do you not know if you guess? Sounds like you're unsure of even what you don't know, you ignorant whelp!" He tried to stand but swayed himself back onto the couch. "You're just lucky my original legs was blowed off in Nam!"

"Dad, I have to tell you something."

"Not until I said all I gotta say, boy. You listen to me! I will not stand for this kind of disobedience in my own place of work!"

After a moment of silence, Chemtrail Chameleon ventured: "Are you finished now?"

"Don't you question me, boy!" The drunk staggered to his feet and charged his son, arms flailing limply.

"Please stop it, dad! You might hurt me!" Chemtrail Chameleon said, barely even feeling his father's feeble blows.

"You're right. I'm sorry," said the old man, coming somewhat to his senses. "I'm just uptight, what with the new job responsibilities and all. Built up a whole shitload of stress, you see." He limped back to the couch and collapsed.

"I'm sorry you're so tense."

"Tell ya what would make me a lot less tense would be a blow job from that sticky tongue of yours."

"Dad, I... that's not right. I won't do it."

"What? Too good for your old man, is ya?"

"No, Dad, I love you, but that is just the liquor talking."

"This is a fucking outrage! No son of mine isn't going to suck my dick! Get out of my sight, you dirty freak. I'll never forgive your mother for stepping into the cloud of CHEMTRAIL when she was pregnant with you! You are getting above your raising, boy! Makes me so mad I could cum in my own son's mouth!"

The lizard boy charged toward the front door, only aware he wanted to be anywhere but his own messed-up home. He slammed the door behind him and hopped on his bike. An Andrew Lloyd Webber across the street cried out, "Whoop-ie-tie-eye-oh!" and waved his Stetson above his head. Chemtrail Chameleon sped to the mall to meet up with Marlon, forgetting about the handful of pistachios in his pocket.

———◆———

Marlon met Chemtrail Chameleon outside the box office of the theater.

"Man, you look upset," Marlon said. "Did someone piss on your baby doll or something?"

"No, dude. It's my dad. He's... you wouldn't understand."

"Fine, with me. I'm a boy so I get real uncomfortable around feelings, like my sisters do around mice. Anyway, this movie is going to kick so much ass you will forget all your worries, man."

"Yeah, I bet so," Chemtrail Chameleon said, perking up.

Both bought tickets and entered the lobby. There was a hairy, chubby guy there wearing an usher's uniform that was too small for him, so tufts of hair shot out, and blobs of fat dripped down around the edges of the uniform.

"Hi, boys. Welcome to the movies," the fat guy said. "Nor-mally, I'd just take your tickets and point you to the correct theater, but I'm afraid we got a really disturbing phone call today."

Chemtrail Chameleon was afraid his father had called and told the theater he was too young to see *Blood Soldier: The Movie*.

"We received a threat."

"Uh...what? Did you get like a bomb threat or something?" Marlon asked.

"No, no, no!" the guy said and chuckled nervously. "We received a very serious treat threat."

The boys looked at him dumbly.

"A treat threat. Someone is planning on smuggling in candy or other snacks. And we can't have that here at the movies. We make our money on concessions."

Marlon snorted sardonically. "Okay. Whatever."

"I'm going to have to pat you boys down," the guy growled lasciviously.

Just as the fat man reached for Chemtrail Chameleon's jean pocket, a nerdy blond teenager dressed only in his underwear came barreling out of a supply closet.

"That man is an impostor!" the blond teen shouted. "He does not work here!" He charged the fat guy and tackled him, somehow managing to pull the hairy beast to the ground.

But the fat man held onto Chemtrail Chameleon's pants pocket tightly, ripping it open and spilling several nuts onto the maroon carpet of the lobby.

Everyone gasped.

"You were treat-smuggling!" the blond teen yelled.

"Yes, he was," the fat guy said, clumsily getting back to his feet. "I'm Agent Spence from the Undercover Perverts division. I'll be taking this boy into custody."

Chemtrail Chameleon tried to run, but was quickly snatched by Spence, who was much quicker than he looked.

As he was dragged away to the torture dungeon where he'd spend the next six months, Chemtrail Chameleon resolved that he would one day change the world for the better by ending ridiculously unjust legal practices such as this. The town police needed to be called to account. It wasn't right to sentence a kid with a few pistachios to months of molestation. One day, he'd make the world see.

———◇———

Twenty-two years later...

The emcee smugly toyed with the audience. "I want to thank Jagged Heresy for opening up the convention tonight. Looking good. Sounding, eh, what's the word, good... *for senior citizens*. Keepin' it metal, guys! Or at least, the two original members who didn't die in that fiery crash so many years ago are keeping it real metal. Let's have a moment of silence for the dead, please."

Some girl with a clipboard and headset signaled that it was almost time.

"And now, without further ado," the emcee said, "I give you this year's nominee!"

Wolf-whistles and furious applause resounded.

Chemtrail Chameleon approached the podium. He was about to deliver the most important speech of his whole presidential campaign.

He cleared his throat, and the PA squealed with feedback for a second, just like you see in all the movies.

"Justice," he said into the microphone. The word echoed around the stadium to a packed crowd, hushed with awe.

"Justice. That's why I decided to run for office. We live in a world where people just don't feel like the system is fair. Those of us up here on stage, the ones making the rules of the game, we've forgotten what common sense is. We've forgotten about the importance of fairness. The common man is more alienated than ever. I bet many of you think, 'Nobody up on that stage is going to give a care about me nohow!' At any other rally, you know what? You'd be right.

"But I've been where you are. I've toiled in the salt mines. I've done my time in the torture dungeons. I know how much you want to give up on so-called political solutions. You just want to drink from your wives' teats, the sweet milk of tranquility.

"I also know you are thinking, 'What's this guy's plan?' I'll tell you what my plan is: fairness. Simple word. Complex plan.

"Take, for instance, a country where the police gun down young black men for sport. Call that fair? Course that's not fair! But you know what, folks? What if the police took that black man they killed so needlessly, cleaned him, cooked him, and used that meat to feed the poor in the community? That sounds fair to me."

The crowd applauded as Chemtrail Chameleon took a sip of water from a Dixie cup.

"And take abortion, as another example. A mother can just cut a poor helpless child out of her body, leave it to die. Call that fair? That's not fair. To make it fair, let's surgically remove that fetus from the womb. Put it in a hyper-incubation chamber, pump it full of steroids and amphetamines. Give it a chainsaw and put it in a fighting arena with the mother. If she can kill that super fetus in a fair fight, then I say that's fair!"

The crowd went wild. Chemtrail Chameleon basked in the moment. For he believed right then that he was going to become the next president.

A gunshot rang out. The crowd froze in terror.

"Hi, I'm Andrew Lloyd Webber, and I'm here to tell you sumpin' bout *fairness*!" said Andrew Lloyd Webber, walking out onto the stage and blowing the smoke from the barrel of his six-shooter.

Chemtrail Chameleon felt the blood running down his forehead and into his gaping mouth. Killed by his own running mate—just like Sgt. Cork had been senselessly blasted to bits by the faceless Cap in that movie he never got to see twenty-two years ago—he had just enough time to reflect on what a poor choice the senile old coot was for VP. Lying on the stage, he gazed up at the papier-mâché image of himself dangling from the rigging on a single wire.

"You were supposed to shoot the piñata."

"Sorry, boy, I don't speak Chinee," said Webber, doing a lasso dance with an invisible rope, really wowing the whole audience.

Marlon, who was working as a roadie for Jagged Heresy, rushed onto the stage and picked up the limp body of his best friend.

"Why!?" he cried.

"Ooopsie!" Webber said, earning a chuckle from the audience.

"Are you at least going to honor his wishes?" Marlon said tearfully. "Clean him, cook him, feed his flesh to these good people! It's the least you can do!"

Andrew Lloyd Webber hung his head and said, "Of course I'm gonna cook him! BBQ-style! What do you think I am? Crazy?"

On the side stage, Jagged Heresy went into an old-school metal rendition of Mexican Radio.

"Plus, I got me some salsa straight out of New York City! Yippee-ki-yay!"

The crowd was never more pleased.

THE STORY OF JOB

When I walk into the supermarket to shop, Job is sure to be one of the first people I run into. This is always to my dismay. Don't get me wrong; I feel pity for the guy. But I can't relate to him, and I guess that's the tragedy of the Mongoloid. I feel about as much of a connection to him as I do to a circus chimp, except I might let the chimp eat off my ice cream cone. Just one lick, but still, I would never let Job anywhere near my food. He exudes error. I don't want to catch the wrongness.

"Hey, Leary!" he calls to me from where he bags at the end of lane six. His shirt is dingy; he's clearly been washing his whites and colors together. I always hope he won't see me, but it's like he's got insect eyes, seeing for nearly 360 degrees, yet they look like little slits.

"Hi, Job," I say with as much false enthusiasm as I can manage at eight in the morning. I try to scurry to the produce department too fast for him to take a real interest, but he's predatory in that regard. My scurrying arouses his appetite for my attention. I pray to my heathen gods that he won't want to touch me. But he's coming my way and holding up his crusty, reptilian mitt because he wants to do a combo high-five/shake. It's something he must have seen in a made-for-TV movie from the Eighties. Whatever grows upon his palms will come in contact with my flesh, but I don't want to be rude, so I make direct skin-on-skin contact. Then I imagine the birth defects that I am liable to pass along to my future offspring, assuming my seed one day finds purchase.

"Hey, Leary!" he says with a warped grin. "Guess what?" And he doesn't give me time to guess; he comes right out with: "I laid more eggs last night, and I hope they are going to hatch this time. The shells are real leathery and scaly, but I'm keeping them warm. When they hatch, I won't call them abominations. I will call them beautiful babies! 'Cause, you know, I got compassion for them, 'cause when I was a baby my mommy tried to throw me back."

I can barely listen. The crudely carven features of his face could be from another epoch. I don't want to look at him anymore, so I say, "Wow, that's tough, Job. Hope your eggs turn out this time. I gotta get shopping." I slink away toward the fruit displays.

"Oh, okay, Leary. I'll catch up with you later."

Haven't we just caught up? I can't quite seem to make his words into sense in my head. I start pawing my way through some pomegranates, but it isn't three seconds before I hear his muddled voice again proclaiming to some other hapless passerby: "You know what I just found out about science? They now know that I am warm-blooded and not cold-blooded like an amphibian. Many scientists now believe my closest relative might be the platypus. You know, with the duck bill." The passerby nods politely and walks away.

I try to fix my gaze on the tropical section, malangas, and kiwanos, but my eyes keep catching glances of Job as he makes his rounds of harassment. I see him talking to a little girl holding a balloon. "You know, I've got a bladder inside me," he says, "a lot like that balloon there. It fills up with air when I get scared, you know, so I look real big to predators who want to eat me." And then he smiles, mouth open, apparently a little too wide. Her father must think the Mongoloid wants to eat his little girl. He pulls out a pistol and puts a bullet right in Job's gut. The howling is unbelievable, like a backroom torture chamber for coyotes. Job falls, forming a pathetic heap upon the freshly waxed floor.

I rush over feeling pity, like I said, not genuine compassion, whatever that means. He's definitely dying. There's enough blood on the floor to cause a serious slipping hazard, so someone pages for a wet clean-up. I didn't expect to see anything like this when I set out for groceries this morning. Job looks me in the face with his yellow eyes. "Leary, don't let me die before I get a chance to see Top Gun 5 in the theater." I hold his coarse, lizard-like hand. I don't have the heart to tell him that Top Gun 5 has already been out of theaters for months and is now available on DVD. It's only a matter of moments until he's gone, and Bill, the black guy who does the floors, shows up.

"Aw, man," Bill says. "We're really short on baggers today." He puts down a wet-floor cone, grabs his push broom, and starts trying to sweep Job out the automatic doors, which takes him a few minutes, but I watch until he pushes the bleeding Mongoloid corpse off the curb. It makes me feel nauseated to watch, more so than when Job was still living. Bill washes his hands in the drinking fountain and goes to work cleaning up the blood-streaked floor.

People are mildly interested as they pass. "Mommy, what's that red stuff?" asks a little boy with a sucker.

"That's how you know the meat is fresh," Mommy says.

Outside, one of the local tribes is already cutting up Job's body to use all his parts. It looks like they are flaying him to use his skin to make into wigwams. I peek out, and they see me, and one says, "Our culture has survived in this manner for hundreds of generations. We can't bear the waste. We will eat his meat, even though Job was always really nice to us and took the time to communicate his innermost thoughts with all the members of the tribe. Did you know his favorite color was fuchsia?" Then he pulls sinews from Job's knees.

No, I had no idea Job even knew what fuchsia was. I want to say this out loud, but for some reason, it doesn't come out. Instead, I say, "That's nice." I feel like the world is a little less full now that they are disemboweling Job in front of the supermarket. The world is less perfect without his imperfection to make it feel like home.

They page for the coroner, but she takes so long to get there that the tribesmen have pretty well shucked Job's corpse already.

"Nothing left of the cadaver. I'll have to do a mock autopsy," says the coroner before she sets up a dummy that, eerily, does look something like a smaller version of Job. She pours red ink on its belly and stands back in contemplation. "Looks like a clear-cut case of bleeding out. The bullet probably hit his gizzard. Not an uncommon cause of death in these Mongoloids. I'll write it up as an accident." That doesn't seem fair, but given the circumstances, I don't know what could be.

There's a moment of awkward silence.

"Someone should probably say something in his honor," I say. And I look at Bill, who is still mopping up blood on the walkway. He just shrugs.

The coroner pushes her glasses up. "I'm not really a good impromptu speaker. Not even extemporaneously good."

So the burden falls to me. I clear my throat: "Dear heathen gods, allow Job's soul, if he has one, which I'm not so sure Mongoloids do—but if he has a soul, let it into Heaven without too much hassle. He wasn't as bad as he could have been. He was the kind of guy that reminded us that we were normal and that we could have it way worse. I will not soon forget his squinty little eyes or thick, rough skin."

"Wait a second," the coroner says as she examines the dummy. "I don't think Job was actually a Mongoloid at all. He probably just had a bad skin condition." She walks away, scribbling something on her chart.

And I look at my hand, and I see the scales forming, and somehow I know that Job will always be with us. As Bill clucks his tongue and hoses what's left of Job into the gutter, I smile a little bit and go inside to start bagging, because they are in dire need of help in there, you know.

THE PITFALLS OF MODERN GARDENING

Ryan's wife Amiga had gone to visit his dead wife Rachel's parents in Syracuse. His first wife had been an only daughter, and her parents liked Ryan, so he felt obligated to send his new wife while he stayed home to take care of a few domestic *issues*.

The yard of Ryan's home had become an uncontrolled wilderness. That's not much of an exaggeration. Amiga blamed Ryan, citing that he was both a man and a lawn care specialist, and so all outdoorsy crafts fell to him by right and by common sense. Amiga's air allergy required that she remain indoors in tightly sealed chambers as much as possible. Ryan was not unreasonable enough to expect her to do any yard work. He was, however, unreasonable enough to buy a large amount of property and let the yard go to brambly, weedy hell. His moustache was perfectly sculpted, and it took a lot of time to keep it that way. This yard situation had come to a head when he and Amiga noticed garden gnomes hosting open mic nights in a makeshift nightclub constructed of brushwood, inviting all sorts of nuisance animals to fraternize there in the undergrowth.

This seemed as good a place to start as any. Ryan asked the bouncer gnome if he could enter and speak with the proprietor. He explained quite reasonably that his back yard was no place for a nightclub, even one for very small patrons, and he really did not care for all the loitering foxes, opossums, and raccoons, which could be carrying that new infection SuperRabies that you hear about on TV all the time.

The bouncer looked him up and down. "Bigot," he said, then did a roundhouse kick that connected with Ryan's shin. It hurt a lot, but Ryan couldn't admit that, though he realized he would need some assistance handling the gnomes. Clearing out the nightclub would have to wait.

There was also the garage. It was a nice, two-car, detached garage like he'd always wanted. Only now it was overgrown with plastic ivy. He took his string trimmer to the fake plants, but it was no use. They were just too tough. He regretted throwing his old Christmas garlands into the backyard, especially when he had regular trash pickup service.

"It would have been very easy to put the old garlands in a garbage can," he said to himself. Instead, he'd allowed them to take root and make his dream garage unusable. He was pretty sure he had a Maserati in there.

Then there was the matter of his vegetable garden. He didn't know if any plants had come up this season because he could not find where the garden was. He did locate some ketchup seed scattered near a large area of brush, so he knew he was getting close. But he wasn't up to the task of hacking through bracken and brambles just to see if his broccoli rabe was salvageable.

Disappointed in himself, Ryan surveyed his yard with dismay and made the only decision a sane man could make: he went inside and fixed himself a strong drink.

He quickly downed a shot of Phoenix Piss, a concentrated derivative of fermented Marmite. The flavor was like the piss of a mythical bird, and it would have to be the piss of a mythical bird because regular birds don't piss. He gasped and then gagged. "It's better than it tastes," he said, quoting the ad slogan.

As Ryan wiped some spittle from his bottom lip, he heard a knock on the side door. He walked up to the door and tried to see out, which was really easy because the door was mostly glass. Outside stood Lindsay, his pregnant, twenty-something neighbor. Her breasts sagged and pendulated, unlike most pregnant breasts Ryan had observed, which were perky and tumescent.

"Hi, Lindsay. What do you want?" he asked through the door.

"Open the door, silly. I need to talk to you about something."

He wasn't sure it was a good idea but let her in anyway.

"Those budgies are at it again," she said. Ryan had heard Lindsay complain about her pet birds before. She was convinced they were gaslighting her. Whenever Ryan had gone over to her house to check on them, they always seemed perfectly normal. "Of course! That's what they want you to think," she'd say.

"Guess what they can do now? They learned to do the beep my phone makes when I have a text message. I'm running around checking my phone all day. It's making me crazy! I can't handle this while being nine and a half months pregnant."

"Whoa, you must be ready to pop."

"Yeah, probably. I keep having these contraction thingees. And it's driving me nuts! I can't take it anymore." She held her belly and huffed.

"Maybe you should go to the hospital."

"No!" she cried, grabbing him by his shirt. "That's just what *they* want."

"I don't know what you expect me to do about your birds, Lindsay," Ryan said, pushing her away.

"One budgie, their leader, can whistle the *Theme from Andy Griffith* all night long. I never sleep, Ryan. Don't you understand? *I never sleep.*"

"Yeah, that sucks. But what do you want me to do about it?"

"Let me sleep in your bed," she said with a wince that pretended to be a smile.

Amiga would not like the idea of Ryan letting a younger woman into their bed, even if she was an extremely pregnant woman who looked like she was about to give birth to a fully grown person.

Ryan firmly but diplomatically stated, "How about I let you take a nap on my couch?"

"Marvelous," Lindsay said and rolled her eyes. She headed for the living room, fiddling with her bra.

"What are you doing?"

"I'm not sleeping in this bra. It's killing my pendulous breasts." She continued to waddle away, leaving Ryan to consider his game plan.

He dragged out an old Yellow Pages and flipped to the lawn care section. Though he himself was a lawn care specialist, he certainly couldn't turn to any of his employees for help on his own lawn. That would be seen as weakness. At any moment, a younger, stronger lawn care specialist might decide to tear out his throat. He had to turn to strangers.

He picked a number from the lawn care list at random and dialed it on his cell phone.

"Uh, hello?" said the voice of an old man.

"Hi," Ryan said. "I need to hire a mechanical assistant to help me wrangle the boscage that is my backyard."

"Huh? Boscage? You should probably call the refuse collectors."

"I mean to say that my yard is quite out of control."

"A'right. What model you want sent out?"

"Something that can chop wood."

"Chop wood? That does sound pretty out of control. You're gonna need a Tin Man, but I gotta tell you, I can't get one out to you before Thursday."

"I need something *today*."

"All I can do today is an Aluminum Man. He's not as tough, but he's all I got."

"Well, if he's all you've got, then send him as soon as you can." Ryan gave the man his address.

"Okay, he'll be over in an hour. And, before you go... What are you more scared of: a monster or a robot?"

"What kinds?"

"Just in general. Overall."

"Evil robots are pretty scary, but there are some truly terrifying monsters."

"Okay, monster it is. Thanks for calling Bobby Billy's Lawn Firm."

The idea of an Aluminum man to assist him did not thrill Ryan. But he hadn't seen one since he was a kid. Maybe they weren't as uncool and stupid as he remembered. In the meantime, he needed to take a crap.

Ryan passed the couch on his way to the bathroom, noticing that Lindsay was tucked up under an afghan, all her clothes in a heap on the floor. He prayed that no other nosy neighbor would peep in and misinterpret the scene. If Amiga got word Lindsay was naked in their home, he'd never hear the end of it.

About twelve minutes passed with him on the toilet. The details of this event are not worth reporting. He stood and flushed and generally felt better about himself because he had set his mind to crapping, and that's what he had done—crapped.

As he exited, he saw that his couch was now empty, except for a rumpled afghan. He turned to look at the floor, hoping there was not still a pile of garments there. His hopes were dashed like sixty meters at an elementary school field day.

Then he heard the scream. Somewhere between blood-curdling and spine-chilling, the scream impressed him. It was a really well-done scream, if conveying utter horror was the goal of the screamer, which, he assumed, it was.

Entering the kitchen, he first saw Lindsay's naked rear end jiggling in terror. She whimpered something that was meant to be words. When he got close enough to see over her shoulder, he noticed a bloody lump of fur on the floor. A dead cat, nearly decapitated.

"Someone killed your poor cat," Lindsay said tremulously.

Ryan tried not to look at her breasts or crotch, but her naked form was so huge he was unsuccessful in his attempts. "We, uh, don't have a cat."

"Who would do this? Who would kill this cat and put it in your kitchen?"

"I have no idea," he said, wondering what to do with the carcass on his floor.

"Ah, I can't look!" She threw herself against him, pressing her head into his shoulder. Her pendulous breasts bounced against his body as she sobbed.

"I think you might feel better if you put some clothes on," he suggested. But he knew it was too late. His clothes were already stained with her nudity and would have to be burned. He would just tell Amiga they got ruined as he battled brush in the yard. But if she were ever to glimpse this shirt, she would see the distinctive imprints of pendulous breasts.

"I'm sorry I'm naked! I can't sleep with clothes on!" she wailed. Ryan had heard that pregnant women were very hormonal, which could result in loud declarative statements.

He patted her on the head like a young child. "There, there," he said.

A phone rang. This was strange, because it sounded like the house phone, but the house phone had died last week. He just hadn't had a chance to bury it yet. To be sure, he checked his cell phone. But it wasn't the cell ringing.

"Aren't you going to get that?" Lindsay asked him.

"Um... phone is dead." But he was already walking toward the wall-mounted phone next to the fridge. It was ringing—rather, a faint mirage of the phone was ringing, vibrating slightly outside the hard lines of his dead phone. "It's the *phone's ghost*." He snatched the phantom receiver and pressed it to his ear.

"Hello, Mr. Jajko," said a squeaky, mechanical voice.

"Hello? Who is this?"

"Uh...." There was a clicking sound, and then a growly, deep monster voice began to speak, "Did you find your *present?*"

"What are you talking about? Who is this?"

"Did you find your dead cat?"

"No, I found *a* dead cat. I don't have a cat."

"Um... what do you mean you don't have a cat? You don't like cats?"

"I like them okay."

"Are you a dog person?"

"No, not really."

"Then why don't you have a cat?"

"I'm allergic, all right! What is it to you?"

"Nothing, nothing. If you are allergic, I guess I understand. But none the less—you found the dead cat. In your kitchen?"

"Yes, I'm looking at its bloody corpse right now."

"And doesn't that scare you? Don't you want to know how it got there?"

"I'm confused why someone else's dead cat is in my kitchen. And yeah, I'm a little disturbed by it. But what is it to you? Did you put it here? Who is this?"

"Questions, questions, questions, Mr. Jajko. Why so many questions? Don't you know who I am?"

"No, I don't know who the hell you are. That's why I asked you."

"Bad things are going to happen to you, Mr. Jajko. *If* you can't solve the riddle."

"Look, first off, I don't find you very funny."

"*I am funny! I am God here!*"

"Just tell me what the hell is going on!"

"Okay, okay," the demonic voice intoned. "Have you ever tried washing a cat in distilled water? You do that a coupla times a month, and it is supposed to cut way down on the allergies. It's the saliva that you are actually allergic to, and if you wash it off—"

"What the fuck are you talking about?"

"Some people just don't know how to handle cats, and it pisses me off."

"Well, evidently, you just killed a random cat for no damn reason, broke into my house, and messed my kitchen floor up! What kind of morality lesson are you going to give me, kitty killer?"

"Kitty killer? Jesus, that's harsh, man. I think you've got me all wrong."

"Then tell me what the fuck you are doing, or I'm calling the cops!"

"Um, never mind. I'll call back later. Keep this line open." *Click*.

"What was all that about?" Lindsay said. She massaged her left tit.

"I have no idea. Do you have to do that in front of me?"

"My boobs hurt! They are getting really swollen. I can't help it! I'm ten months pregnant." She stormed into the living room.

He thought the dead cat looked like Old Man Harkins' tabby, Noodle Pie. It wasn't rare that Ryan caught Noodle Pie rooting around in his garbage. Harkins was an old-school farm type—probably didn't feed the cat regularly. There was no way Ryan was going to tell the man his little tabby friend was deceased, a victim of felicide. Ryan tossed the cat in a tall kitchen trash bag, poured some bleach on the floor and grabbed his mop. The blood was still fresh, so cleanup was relatively easy. As he mopped, he wondered if he was in danger. Someone, even if it wasn't the creepy monster-man who had called him on the ghost phone, had snuck into his home and left a very morbid message for him.

He popped outside to toss the bag of cat in the trash can and noticed that there was a shiny, metallic figure walking down the road. It had to be the Aluminum Man. At the rate he was going, he would be there in several minutes. Ryan started to forget all about the cat, setting his mind back to important matters like clipping weeds and chasing away gnomish businesses.

Then he heard another scream. This one was a scream of pain, though, and not as well done as the previous scream. He ran to the living room.

"It's time! I'm giving birth!" Lindsay yelled from the floor. The carpet was already smeared with blood and bodily waste. "Finally, after ten and a half months, it's coming out! It's okay, though. I took Lamaze." She alternately huffed, puffed, and grunted.

"Don't you need, like, a partner or something for that?"

"Not if you are *good* at it! Ahhhhhh!" Sweat beaded on her forehead as she fell into a regular breathing pattern. A moment of Zen came over her.

He watched in awe. She was *very* good at it.

"I have a dream for this baby. I will enter her into a contest," she said calmly. "I want her to take second place—Second Best Baby. Some people tell me, don't go for Second Best Baby, but I say first place has too many responsibilities heaped on. So no—only second best for my baby."

"That makes sense, I guess," Ryan said, only having half-heard her blather.

There was a clank at the door.

"Come in!" Ryan called, trying not to panic. He wished that he knew Lamaze.

A clunking sound preceded the appearance of a man constructed of glinting, flimsy metal. His body looked like an old Franklin stove, and the top of his head looked like a funnel. He carried a hatchet, and his mouth was a smiling bear trap.

"I am the Aluminum Man sent to aid you with your gardening needs. You may call me Pinkerton." His voice was even and pleasant. He looked from Ryan down to Lindsay. "This does not look like a gardening concern."

"Do you know anything about birthing babies?" Ryan asked him.

"Truth to tell, that is what the Aluminum Men were designed for."

Lindsay was still in her zone, but it was clear to Ryan that she struggled.

"Something is wrong," said Pinkerton. "I will have a look." He got on his knees, set down his hatchet, and peered into the birth canal. "There is a big problem here. I don't know if I can help her."

"What? What do you mean?" Ryan said.

"It is an irregular pregnancy."

"Yes, she said she was over ten months along."

"She is much farther along than that," said Pinkerton, standing and stepping back.

Blood poured forth from her vagina as a large hand emerged. Lindsay's face contorted and a shriek broke forth from her throat.

"What's going on?" Ryan shouted.

"She's dying," Pinkerton said.

The creepily large hand pawed around, tearing at its mother's body. Gradually another hand slithered out, and the two hands began to part the birth canal. Lindsay stopped screaming and just lay there, dazed, drifting off into nothing.

A head emerged. Long, bloody hair covered the face, which looked like an elderly version of Lindsay. The old baby made a sound somewhere between a dog growl and the buzzing of an insect. Unlike its naked mother, the newborn wore an old lady nightgown. With half the torso emerged, the old baby began to bite into its mother's legs, eating her while she was still partially alive.

"Is this normal?" asked Ryan.

"It is normal for old babies," Pinkerton said, leaning down to pick up his hatchet. "But old babies are not normal. In fact, they are abominations. I will have to cut this one open."

The old baby was now fully born. It squatted in a spider-like stance and skittered, legs stepping over shoulders, arms slithering forward. Ryan backed away as Pinkerton stalwartly stood his ground. The Aluminum Man raised his hatchet. The old baby turned to consume the rest of its dying mother, who looked like a half-deflated pool toy. The blade came down on the crooked back. A low, demonic groan emanated from the deep wound stretching across most of the torso. Strangely, there was no blood. But after Pinkerton pulled the weapon back, the body continued to split down the middle, breaking into nearly perfect halves.

"It is doubtful the old baby will survive this," Pinkerton said to Ryan, who simply stood and stared.

"Are you all right, Mr. Jajko?" the Aluminum Man asked.

"Yeah, it's just that I used to date this girl who had a fetish about being cut in half. It always seemed so impossible."

"It is not easy," Pinkerton admitted, "but it can be done."

Lindsay was now still, no signs of life. The old baby lay split in half atop its mother's corpse. It was a mess. The bodies would not fit in a tall kitchen trash bag.

"You figured out the riddle yet, Mr. Jajko?" said a deep, eerie monster voice that seemed to originate within the dead baby.

The remains wriggled, then a small hole was punched in the old baby's back by a gray feline paw. A tabby cat shot out, sending bits and pieces of dead old baby spray all over Pinkerton's face and into Ryan's gaping mouth. The dead flesh tasted of mothballs and woolen mittens. The cat landed on all fours at Ryan's feet and looked up, as if expecting to be fed.

"Noodle Pie? But if you are here, who is in my trash can?"

"Why don't you go have a look?" said the cat in its monstrous voice.

"I don't understand...."

"Mr. Jajko, collect yourself and go look in the trash."

Ryan walked slowly, zombie-like, even sticking his arms out in front in case he tripped and fell over. He felt light-headed. He felt nauseated. He felt glad that he wasn't doing yard work. When he reached the trash can, he opened the lid hesitantly, like something might jump out and get him.

Nothing jumped out.

He reached in cautiously and fished out the tall kitchen bag. He ripped it open and let the cat fall to the ground. It was a gray tabby. But it was wearing a pink collar. A pink collar with a tag that said *Amiga*.

"She never made it to your old in-law's place," said Pinkerton from the open side door.

Tears formed in Ryan's eyes. "But why? Who?"

"It was those gnomes, Ryan. You know what you have to do," said Noodle Pie, nuzzling against the back of his leg.

"What in the name of hell is goin' on here?" said the voice of an old country black man.

Ryan turned to find the source. "Mr. Harkins... I didn't see you there."

"Ryan, I know you been havin' an affair with that Lindsay girl. You think nobody peepin' on you? *Think again*. You put a baby on up in there, yes you did. Then you killed your wife and you killed your mistress and you killed your baby! I'm a-callin the 'thorities!"

Ryan tried to say something, but what could he say? He had no idea what was happening.

"I will stop him, Mr. Jajko," said Pinkerton. He sent his hatchet flying, spinning right into the center of the aged man's skull. Again, the split did not stop there. The entire body of the man trembled and cleaved in half. As the flesh fell away to each side, Lindsay was revealed. Naked but no longer pregnant. She was covered in a pinkish goo that she licked from her body like a cat cleaning herself.

"I'm going to need some fucking therapy," Ryan said.

"Truth to tell, Aluminum men are made to administer Freudian psychoanalysis. But you are going to need something more Jungian."

"I want you in my pussy, Ryan," Lindsay said, and she pointed to her lady parts as if there might be some confusion.

"Oh, no you don't, bitch!" screamed Amiga, who wasn't really dead at all, but had the talent of making it look like she'd been nearly decapitated. It was a great party trick, and she'd done it the night she met Ryan.

"I totally forgot she could do that," said Ryan, feeling slightly less sad, but much more confused.

Amiga leapt in a great arc, doing a spin kick in midair. Her paw caught Lindsay right in the eye, popping it loose. The orb dangled from nerves and tendons stretched almost to the ground, and both cats began to bat her eyeball around, playing a sort of feline tether ball.

"Congrats, Amiga! This was your best idea ever," said Noodle Pie in the monster voice.

"You can stop doing the voice now," said Amiga.

"Just what the fuck is going here?" Ryan said, wagging his finger at his cat wife.

"I'm just teaching you a lesson. Never send your new wife to spend time with your dead wife's family. Or the new wife might end up dead, haunting you from beyond the grave, but disguised as some other ghost as revenge. Something like that. It sounded better when we were planning it."

"Well, who the hell is this Aluminum Man? What's he got to do with it?"

"I'm just an actor," said Pinkerton. He removed his head, to reveal a face that looked just like Ryan, except without a moustache. "Your wife hired me a couple of days ago."

Ryan hung his head and started shaking rhythmically.

"It's okay, baby," Amiga said, rubbing up against his legs. "I've taught you enough for one day. Things can go back to normal now."

But he wasn't sobbing. He was laughing. His laughing grew to a hideous crescendo. "Well, if you are all in the mood for confessions, I guess I have one too." He reached up and ripped his mustache away. "I'm just an actor too! Hired by Ryan when he was just an infant to play himself! I've had you all fooled *for years*! I'll be collecting my Emmy now."

The others gasped. Amiga started coughing because she'd been in the open air so long that her allergy was really acting up.

One-eyed Lindsay was the first to speak. "Well, if you aren't Ryan, then where is the real Ryan?" Awkwardly, she attempted to jam her eye back in the socket, but she left a bit of tendon hanging down like a fleshy tear drop.

"I've got an idea about that," said the Non-Ryan.

He took the others into the backyard, explaining about the gnome nightclub. "The way I see it, if we put on pointy hats and walk on our knees, they'll totally let us in."

So, the two actors, Lindsay, and the two cats, got on their knees and put on dunce caps. They walked right up to the bouncer gnome, and the Non-Pinkerton said, "We are just some gnomes looking for a good time."

"Oh yeah?" the bouncer asked.

"You know where we can find some fun?" Non-Ryan said.

"I don't know what you tall-ies do for fun, but maybe you can go sit on highchairs or shoot some hoops. And take those stupid hats off! Scram!"

"Why don't you stuff it, runt!" yelled Noodle Pie.

"Go burry your turds, fish-bone picker!" yelled the bouncer.

"Gentlemen, gentlemen!" said another small person standing at the club entrance. He looked more like a baby than a gnome, but he had a distinctive moustache. "There is no need to squabble. Glitrick," he said to the bouncer, "these are my long-awaited guests."

Glitrick the bouncer looked down in shame. "I'm sorry, Ryan, I didn't know these big'uns belonged to you. My bad."

"Your bad indeed!" baby Ryan scolded. He looked at the group with a glint in his eye. "If you will all please join me in the atrium." He motioned for them to enter. They followed him past the line of bushes that protected the club from the exterior yard, and into an elaborate candlelit hall, and still past that into what looked like a giant, hollowed-out heart.

"Have a seat, all of you, please."

Each took a seat on chairs designed to look like hemoglobin molecules.

"I would like a chance to explain myself," Ryan began. "I know some of you will never understand my actions. Others of you will pretend to understand, but secretly judge me. Others of you might judge me to my face, like judging judgers."

Lindsay giggled, causing her pendulous breasts to swing side to side.

"Some of you," he continued, "will think me a madman. Some may even proclaim me a genius. Others will think this is all a set-up for an elaborate reality television program. Others will think I'm stupid. Some may even claim that I was hit on the head with a large mallet when I was just a pup, no higher than an ant's eye."

"Is there a point to any of this?" Noodle Pie said.

Ryan cleared his throat. "Some may not see the point in what I've done. Others may see the point but pretend to not." He breathed deeply. "All this is to say, I love you, Amiga. I've had to hire a man to play me because I feel totally inadequate to fulfill your needs, both sexually and in relation to gardening."

Amiga wished she could weep, but she was a cat, so she closed her eerie inner eyelid instead. "I love you too, Ryan. I'm amazed by what trouble you've gone through to keep me happy."

"And I, too, am astonished by the lengths you've gone to perplex the actor that plays me in the relationship. For that, I am eternally grateful to both you and to Paul."

"Who is Paul?" asked Amiga.

"I'm Paul," said the actor formerly known as Ryan.

"Yes, you really did an exceptional job. I can't believe how lifelike and brushable your hair is," Amiga purred.

"If no one objects," the real Ryan said, "I would like to return home with the two of you. We can form a family triad. We will have everything we need for success."

"That sounds nice," Amiga said with a cat-smile.

"The rest of you can fuck off, now. Get the hell out of my club!" Ryan said to Lindsay, Noodle Pie and Non-Pinkerton. "What are you waiting for? Go!"

"Christ, don't be such a douchebag, dude!" said Lindsay.

"Don't listen to her, baby! *Do* be a douchebag!" cheered Amiga.

"Yeah, get the fuck out of here!" Paul said.

The three of them jeered until the other three stood and left the atrium. Once they were alone, they embraced.

"I never thought it could be like this," they all said at exactly the same time. "It's like you are reading my mind! This is the best thing ever!"

And that's how relationships work. Don't let anybody tell you otherwise.

HARBINGER MASTER

Bark and Drip sat in the beat-up Celica, talking about who was more important: Fudge Tunnel or Buzzov*en. The parking lot outside Danger Daddy's Rock Club was lit by a couple of yellow streetlights, the smell of soured beer creeping out of the off-green dumpster a few spots over from Bark's crappy car. Drip wore his Eyehategod longsleeve. Bark wore a Melvins tee, but only because he could not find his Destripper Klaw shirt. That's who they came to see tonight. DK was the best local sludgecore band. On this point, Drip and Bark both agreed.

"*Hate Songs* was out, like, two years before *To a Frown*," Bark said.

"Dude, I know how time works," Drip said. "I didn't say Buzzove*en was *before* Fudge Tunnel. I said they were *better*. Learn the goddamn difference."

A lot of people mistook the two for brothers. They both had the same long, ashen hair. They both had the same oily teenage complexion and black plastic-frame glasses. They both wore almost exclusively black. They both had the same taste in music and liked all the same barbarian, horror, and sci-fi movies. Drip and Bark merely ranked them slightly differently, leading to rambling argumentation hours most nights.

But not tonight.

"I know, man. I don't want to get into it right now. Let's just go get our hands X'd and get a good spot to watch Destripper Klaw," said Bark.

"Holy shit, this is going to be a great night, dude. Hey, who's opening up for them?" Drip said.

"Um, some band from PA called Harbinger Master," Bark said. "I asked Metal Jim if he'd heard them, and he said all he knew was they have, like, a Chinese girl that sings, and they alternate fast beats with slow, groovy breakdowns. But it's not typical hardcore. He said he couldn't explain it. He tried to hold the phone up to the speaker of his boom box while he played me part of the demo, but it just sounded like tinny static over the phone."

"Is the chick supposed to be hot?"

"He said she looks super young, and the three dudes look like total geeks."

"God, I hate it when metal dudes look like geeks," said Drip, pushing his glasses up with index finger. He opened his door and got out of the car. "Man, I wish I had some of those beedies that Vernon smokes."

"I thought you hated smoking?" Bark said, following suit and locking the car doors.

"Regular cigarettes are so gay, but those beedies taste awesome, man. They are, like, spicy."

"You could always smoke menthols," Bark joked.

They strode to the door with a sense of purpose, about to enter the coolest metal club in town.

Inside, the place was nearly barren. They wandered up to the bar, where only one other person was currently standing.

"I know it's still early, but there should be more people here for Destripper Klaw," said Drip.

"DK canceled," the other guy said. He was a few years older, probably just barely twenty-one. In one of his hands was a lit clove; in the other, a bottle of cheap domestic beer. He had shortish dirty-blonde hair and was dressed in a Danzig t-shirt, black jeans, and dirty black Converse.

"No fucking way!" said Bark, slamming his palms down on the bar.

"The door guy didn't say anything about that. What a rip-off!" Drip said.

"Harbinger Master is still playing, though," the guy said, then took a long tug off his beer.

"We've never heard them. Are they any good?" Bark said.

The guy scoffed and said, "Yeah, only the best band out of Harrisburg."

"I've never even heard *any* bands from Harrisburg," Drip said.

"Yeah, well, it's not that big of a music town. Still, *Harbinger Master rules*," the guy said, sounding a little impatient.

"Are you, like, friends with them?" Drip said.

"I'm the bass player," the guy said.

"Oh, that's cool," said Bark.

"I play a five-string. We tune down pretty far, but that doesn't mean I don't play the shit out of the thing. We aren't just like *root note, pull-off, root note* bullshit. Too much of that crap." He took a drag of his clove.

"Yeah, we play a little bit too," said Bark, brushing his hair out his eyes.

"What kind of stuff do you play?" the guy asked, staring right at Bark. The question was asked so quickly that it put Bark on the spot, and he stuttered before Drip took over.

"Uh, mainly covers right now," said Drip. "Some Crowbar, some Samhain, some Helmet, some Clutch."

"No offense, but that shit is lame. Covers are for losers who can't think of cool riffs themselves. Like, in the last ten seconds, I just thought of five or six awesome bass licks that I can't wait to use. Shit, yeah, now that I think about it, I've got a whole new song in my head right now. Duh-duh-da-duh," he said, beginning to imitate the sound of his bass guitar. "And I think I'll use my fuzz box on this one, really crank it up, get a rumbling buzz going on. See how easy that is? I only respect people who write their own stuff, no offense, kids."

"I mean, we totally want to start writing our own stuff, but we don't have a steady drummer or singer yet," said Drip.

"Wait—you guys like Bolt Thrower?" the guy said.

"Um, um, yeah, totally. They rule," said Drip. Bark nodded agreement.

"*The IVth Crusade* might be the best album ever. Duh-duh-da-duh," he began to imitate a bass again, presumably a Bolt Thrower riff, but it sounded the same as the one he mimicked before. "I can't believe you love BT as much as I do. You kids are pretty cool. You should come hang out with us before we go on."

"Okay, that's cool," said Drip. Bark's eyes widened.

The guy ground out his clove in a small aluminum ashtray and walked toward a black door in the back, with the words STAY OUT stenciled on.

"I'm Clint, by the way," he said without turning around. He opened the door, and the two followed him up a dilapidated, dimly lit stairway. "The lounge is on the third story."

"I didn't realize this place had a third story," Bark said, finally finding the courage to speak again.

"This building," Clint said, "was originally going to be, like, a part of some insane rich guy's giant pleasure palace for gay sex. Like, he was going to attach a bunch of buildings with tunnels all around the city. And there were going to be all these sky walkways, so he could enter from the top levels of the building too. Imagine, walking around on the street and looking up at these weird, enclosed walkways leading to different buildings and knowing there was some rich old pervert dude probably walking right on top of your head."

"Where'd you find out about that?" said Drip.

"From Sooter, he owns this place. Anyway, the point I was making was that the top floor is all done up real fancy in sort of an old fruity style, and Sooter doesn't like to let just anybody up here. It is reserved for VIPs. Do you know what that is?"

"Like princesses and movie stars and diplomats?" said Bark.

"Well, yeah. But that's also excellent bands like Harbinger Master and their select guests. So tonight, boys, you are VIPs. Unless you start bugging me or some shit and then I will not hesitate to send you back downstairs. No offense, but I hate annoying motherfuckers that get on my nerves real bad."

Bark and Drip just stared at him silently as they finished the ascent. The top floor was carpeted in burgundy with a gold latticework pattern. A short corridor led to a heavy oak door with a brass plaque on it that said PENTHOUSE in a bold sans serif font. Clint knocked three times, paused, and knocked four more times.

"Secret knock," he said to the younger boys.

A click came from the deadbolt and the door opened to reveal a short but stout black man dressed like a leprechaun with dark aviator sunglasses. His dreadlocks reached his waist, and he had a knobby stick with a bulbous head he held like a cane.

"Oh," the man grunted. "It's you. Begorrah! Who be these other two? Hooligans galore, be assured, I'll whack you right in the noggins with my shillelagh if you crack wise, now. Dash you right to smithereens! I'm no phony! I'll rock your worlds, little rockers!" His voice was comically high-pitched, and the accent sounded more like a pirate than an Irishman.

"It's okay, Kilkirk," Clint said, "these guys are with me. They're cool. I checked them out."

Kilkirk sneered and shook his head. He raised the shillelagh to point at the lounge. "Right this way... *gentlemen*."

The three shuffled in as the small man led the way.

"You know, I used to cater to the whims of European noblemen, Arab caliphs, Russian boyars."

"Dude, what the fuck is a boyar?" asked Clint. "Like, a pederast or something, is that what you mean?" He promptly laughed at his own joke.

"Nothing of the sort. More like dukes."

"You totally let them fuck you and pretend you were a young boy! Admit it, dude."

Kilkirk turned and scowled at Clint, but since they had reached the lounge area, the little man excused himself and returned to the door. There were several elegant armchairs and sofas arranged around a glass coffee table. Seated were two guys and a girl—obviously the other members of Harbinger Master.

"Who brought the kinnygardners?" a fat, acne-scarred guy with long, stringy black hair said with a snort. He wore a Godflesh t-shirt and held a drumstick in each hand. The other guy, wearing a skull and crossbones bandanna and Paradise Lost hoodie, chuckled and took a sip of his Natty Boh.

"I met these guys downstairs," Clint said. "They are cool, and I told them they could hang with us."

"Who they are names?" the girl asked in broken English. She was stunningly beautiful with high cheekbones and unblemished golden skin, her hair dyed bright magenta. She could have been fifteen or much older—there was an air of sophistication about her that made it impossible to tell. The black and silver pleather outfit she wore was skintight.

"Everyone calls me Bark. Last name's Barker."

"I'm Doug, but you can call me Drip."

"Ah...," she said quizzically. "I sorry. I don't talk you." She began reading from a fashion magazine.

"Ichigo's English isn't so good," Clint said under his breath. "But her voice is like a dying angel made out of, like, spare machine parts with sharp edges, covered in toxic ooze. She totally rules."

"How old is she?" asked Bark.

"Why, dude? You wanna date her?"

"Uh, no, I just... she looks young, is all."

"All Orientals look young when they are young. It's, like, from their genes," Clint said. He tossed a clove into his mouth and cupped his hand as he lit it.

"But seriously," Drip said. "How old is she?"

"A lot older than you guys, and out of your league, no offense, but you are kind of dorks, and she's pretty hot."

"And she's Chinese?" Bark said.

"She's fucking Japanese, asshole. Learn the difference," Clint said.

The girl did not look up from her magazine.

"Yeah, you ignorant bozos!" yelled the fat guy with the drum sticks.

"Hey now," Clint said, "these dicks are my new buddies. They love Bolt Thrower, so don't start dumb shit with them, Leon."

"Fine. I'm just messing with you guys," Leon said and tapped his thighs rapidly with the drumsticks, simulating machinegun fire.

"You guys want something to drink?" said the guy in the bandana, rising and heading toward the bar. He had a European accent that sounded a little spooky.

"Oh, we're underage," said Drip.

"You look twenty-one to me," said the guy, grabbing two cans of beer and tossing them to the boys.

"Wow, thanks, man!" said Bark.

"Name's Kesimir," he said.

"Have a seat, boys," Clint encouraged, slouching onto a loveseat.

The boys eyed each other warily and then sat together on a divan, careful to leave plenty of room between them. Bark drank his beer and looked at Drip. There was a long awkward silence. The three guys in the band were staring at them, not menacingly but disconcertingly nonetheless.

"So, uh, what do you guys think of *Far Beyond Driven*?" Drip said.

Leon scoffed.

"I don't listen to much American shit," Kesimir said, crushing his empty Boh can against the coffee table.

"Pantera is like a weak version of *Slayer* or *Sepultura*," Clint said. He took a drag off the clove and blew small smoke rings.

"I kinda liked the direction they were going," said Drip.

"They are just a lame hair band who accidentally saw some New York Hardcore bands and decided to be badasses. Fuck that. Their lyrics are so fucking ridiculous. Might as well just be reading from Nietzsche."

Bark and Drip were too shocked to reply.

"Rule of thumb, guys. There are only three American Metal bands that it is okay to like: Slayer, Danzig..." Clint paused a long time for dramatic effect. Too long.

"What's the third?" Drip asked.

"And Harbinger Master, of course."

The band members all laughed, and the boys gradually joined in.

"Oh, so you are just pulling our leg about all this," Drip said with relief.

"No, fucking no way," Clint said seriously. "Pantera is shitty, and so are most American bands. It's just a fact. Europe is like twenty years ahead in terms of Metal. Have you guys heard Corpse Labyrinth out of Belgium? Or Forgotten Oblivion from Austria? Captive of Butterfly from Luxembourg? Or Curse of the Crash from Andorra? No, because you are too busy gumming up your brains with American bullshit!"

"I like Entombed," said Drip meekly.

"Yeah," Clint said passively, "Entombed are pretty good. But not as good as League of The Troll, another great Swedish band."

"I like best Japanese band T. Rex II: Electric Day Man," said Ichigo. "They cover only T. Rex with electro-death sound. Big metal!" She screamed and held up two horned hands.

"So basically, American music is for pussies," said Kesimir.

Bark scrunched his brow and cast a sidelong glance at Drip. Drip cleared his throat and said, "Uh, so you guys going to be touring soon?"

"No," Clint said. "I won't have the time for that since I'm working on my new novel. It's called *Massive Fucking Attack of the Heavy Metal Monkeys.*"

The boys laughed. But a narrowing of the eyes indicated Clint was not joking.

"What's it about?" indulged Bark.

"Basically, it's the tale of a teenage metalhead who buys a Massive Attack album assuming it's going to be brutal Heavy Metal only to find it's the complete opposite. Massive Attack are some kind of music from England called Trip Hop, which basically means it's like music for fags to do drugs to. So the kid is pissed, I mean *pissed*. He transforms into a Heavy Metal Monkey to find them and seek revenge."

"What's a Heavy Metal Monkey?" asked Drip.

"Basically, like a super badass baboon with all kinds of studded wristlets and shoulder pads straight out of *Road Warrior*. He wears a helmet made out of a human skull, stained with the blood of a virgin goat.

"And each genre of music produces their own monkey armies, dude, so there are Punk Monkeys, Industrial Monkeys, Goth Monkeys, Hardcore Monkeys... even Jazz Monkeys."

"Jazz Monkeys?" scoffed Leon, still beating his legs with his sticks.

"Yeah, of fucking course Jazz Monkeys. The kid even encounters a group of Jazz Monkeys, and he thinks he can easily take them until he realizes these are no ordinary Jazz Monkeys. Theses are *G. Monkeys*."

"You mean...?" Drip said.

"Yes, hardcore fans of Kenny G. They even have his weird kinky long hair and clubs fashioned from those straight saxes he plays. The *G* stands for Gorelick. That's his real last name. *GORE-LICK*... of course his fans are going to be extreme. And that motherfucker is from Seattle! He could kick Alice in Chains' asses any day of the fucking week.

"But the story really gets complicated when the kid meets up with a much older Heavy Metal Monkey who had had a similar experience in the 80s with the band Glass Tiger, who he expected to have wailing shred guitar solos, but instead were just New Wave from Canada. The old guy spent a lot of time tracking down his prey and studying the band's habits, and he found that these trickster false Metal bands employ special anti-monkey sorcerers to protect them from vengeful listeners. The kid knows he's going to have his work cut out for him, so he seeks out the Monkey Heart, a hidden temple at the center of the zoo where all monkey lore has been kept by Darwin's mummy for millions of years."

"That sounds absolutely fucking crazy," said Drip.

"Thanks, man. This will be my ninth book. Six novels, two novellas, and one shorts collection called *Disemboweling Kittens with a Pocket Watch.*"

"Where can we buy a copy?" said Drip.

"I don't write for other people," said Clint walking toward the bar. "I'm not a sellout. No publisher could handle my cosmic jive anyway. The books are just for me. But, you know, maybe someone will find them and publish them after I die or something. Who knows."

He came back from the bar with a fancy wine bottle encircled in pewter snakes with batwings. In his other hand, he held some Dixie cups. He set them all out on the coffee table, nine of them, and poured a bit of dark red liquid into each cup.

"Okay, enough chitchat. Let's get down to the toast," he said, setting down the bottle with a *clink*. Each of the band members grabbed a cup, and the boys followed. Kilkirk swaggered up and grabbed another, leaving two on the table.

"Who are the others for?" Drip asked.

"One would be for me, I hope," said a lisping voice from behind them. The boys turned to see a shadowy figure standing in a doorway in the wall just past the bar. A frail, bald man emerged, dressed in a smoking jacket. He walked stiffly using a cane. Raising his pencil moustache at one side, he smirked at Drip and Bark. Then he winked at them. "And the other will be for my bodyguard, Chemosh."

"Where's he at?" asked Drip.

"He is with me always," said the man, and the boys could now see the deep lines on his face. He looked two hundred years old at least, feebly bending to pick up a paper cup of red liquid. "You can't always see him, unless he wants you to. He's a barghest."

"Boys, meet Sooter," announced Clint in a semi-official tone.

"You own this place?" Bark asked.

"Built it, even," said Sooter with a snaggle-toothed grin. "I had big plans for a Temple of Hedonism, but the locals didn't cotton to my free-thinking ways. They didn't want me having my orgies with my fagot friends. And they nearly shit their pants when they saw how fucking queer I was. I told them to go finger their wives' pussies if I threatened their uptight patriarchy that much. First time I appeared in public in my assless chaps, they came out with pitchforks and torches. Regular horror show." The old man laughed like a drunk donkey, so the boys chuckled nervously.

"Oh, Chemosh, have a cup of sauce," Sooter said gently.

A dark, hulking form was visible for just a split second, a smoky humanoid shape with apelike arms and an elongated snout like a crocodile. Around its body were heavy chains. It picked up the cup then vanished, making it appear that the container was hovering in midair.

Bark yelped, and Drip gaped.

Sooter laughed again until he began a dry fit of hacking coughs.

"Gentlemen and lady, to a night of mystical evil," said Clint. Everyone but the boys tossed back the drinks without hesitation and stared at the cups left undrunk.

"Tsk-tsk. I thought you were going to choose wisely this time, Clinton," Sooter said, shaking his head. "These boys are fearful and ignorant of the Ways of the Perverse Nights."

"Drink your drinks, boys," said Kesimir, sternly, imperiously. A disturbing glint flashed in his eye.

Bark looked into his cup. It looked like blood, but it didn't smell like blood. Drip glanced at him and nodded. They both downed the substance, thick and salty and chemical.

"Gooble gabble, gooble gabble!" chanted Leon.

"I hope we don't get AIDS from that," Drip joked.

"AIDS?" Sooter said. "Oh, I shouldn't think so. They boil it or something first, right Clint?"

"Yes, you old queen. We boil the shit out of that shit."

Drip's eyes became heavy, and he fell back into his seat. Bark's knees buckled and he crouched down.

"What did we drink?" Drip said.

"The Essence of Evil, lads. The Sauce of Satan. Have patience. All will be revealed in good time."

———◦———

Bark roused from his stupor to find himself tied to an armchair. At least he *felt like* he was tied to the chair, but as he assessed his body, he could not locate any bonds. Drip was next to him in another chair, also starting to stir. They were both now dressed in black robes. The others, also in robes, stood in front of them in a semicircle, the room lit by candlelight.

"What's going on? Where's my clothes?"

"Pshaw! There shall be no need of mortal garments this e'en," said Sooter flamboyantly. "Tonight is but for communal ceremonies of the spiritual flesh."

"Why can't I move?"

"Your mind believes you can't. Until I command it, you must remain still. This is done purely as a safety precaution for your own benefit. The air is full of daevas and lemures, manes and oni."

"What?"

"Fucking powerful spirits, dude," said Clint.

"The spirits wish to have congress with your neophytic dicks," said Sooter with a giggle. "So many hungry homos from the world beyond the mortal plane. The otherside is a wild ride. It's totally fucking gay! Bask in the wickedly homosexual rays of man-sin and grow strong!"

"You are crazy!" cried Drip.

"Let us go!" pled Bark.

A chorus of ghostly voices issued forth a diabolical chant from somewhere in the recesses of the room.

"Fuckin' A!" Leon said to Clint. "Soundtrack from Malus Malevolencius III. Rad, dude. I didn't even know it had been released on CD. Good choice."

"It's from fucking part IV, dumbass," sneered Clint.

Drip and Bark looked fearfully on in disbelief.

"Now," said Sooter, pulling back his hood to reveal his pate glistening in the light of ceremonial candles. "Bark, Drip... we must ask of you two a sacrifice to his Holilessness, Lecheron the All-Sexing.

Kilkirk stepped forward, a serpentine dagger in each fist. The small man's eyes obscured by the hood. His bared teeth glinted as he plodded forth, drawing out their agony.

"We hate to ask this of you, having only just met you," said Kesimir. "But we need blood tonight, boys. You must give us blood."

"No! Don't do this!" screamed Bark. "I'm only seventeen! I've never even gotten to third base!"

Leon laughed. "Pussy!"

Kilkirk bent forward, the blades nearing the boys' hearts.

"It is time," said Sooter solemnly, "For the two of you to... kill Kilkirk."

The small man swiftly and deftly reversed the knives so that the handles were now within easy reach of the boys.

"It's okay, lads. It is me time to bleed."

Now free of its magical restraints, Bark moved his arm and took the blade.

Drip stammered, "No, no, no way. I'm not killing anyone."

Kilkirk laid himself prone at their feet.

"It's all right, me boy. Just cut me once. Your friend can finish me off."

"Kill him! Bleed him! Kill him! Bleed him!" chanted the members of Harbinger Master.

"It's him or you," said Kesimir.

"Raaaaaaah!" screamed Bark, sinking his blade deep into an eyeball.

Kilkirk squealed in pain, then broke into mad cackling. Bark backed away.

Drip dropped his knife and hid his eyes.

"Just cut the little man, child, and then we will let you go," Sooter said.

"No, no, never!" Drip dropped to the floor and hugged his knees to his chest, rocking like a mental patient.

"Someone fucking finish me! Oh, and Begorrah!"

Kesimir threw back his head and howled animalistically, then ran toward the small man, scooped him up, and snapped his jaws into his tiny throat. Blood gushed forth, and Kilkirk gurgled weakly. Kesimir shook his head side to side, tearing away bits of flesh and sinew with snaps that caused Drip to throw up down his front.

"Are you a fucking vampire?" Bark said.

"No, you fucking racist," said Clint. "You think he's a vampire just because he's Eastern European?"

"No, I think because he biting out a guy's throat, he's a vampire," said Bark.

"Fuck no. He's a pricolici."

"What's a pricolici?" asked Drip, wiping some of the vomit from his lower lip.

"Shit," said Clint with a shrug. "Sort of like a vampire. Also kind of a werewolf. I don't know, dude."

Kesimir dropped Kilkirk's desiccated form to the floor like a ragdoll. His face was almost entirely blood-soaked.

"Holy fuck, dude! That was rad!" said Leon.

Bark slid over next to Drip and helped him stand.

"Okay, Kilkirk's dead. Can we go now?"

"I believe the deal was that you both needed to draw his blood," said Sooter. "Drip, I'm so disappointed in you. Now you will have to suffer one further ordeal."

"No, please no," Drip muttered.

"You must now fuck Ichigo," announced Sooter. "It is her fertile time. Act as a vehicle for demonseed."

"Wait, I had to stab a guy to death, and *he gets to fuck a hot Asian girl?*" Bark said.

"Oh, dude. That so sucks for you," said Clint, patting Bark on the shoulder, "especially since you just told us all you are a virgin."

Leon laughed so hard he snorted.

"Drip's a virgin too!" Bark said.

"Um, actually not anymore. Remember that night I slept over, and your sister kept walking around in her underwear?"

Bark's eyes grew dark with hatred. He lunged at Drip, roundhouse punch connecting with the other boy's jaws. Drip's head flipped back, then jerked forward again as he spat blood all over Bark. Rage welled within the blood-covered boy, but he was pushed away from Drip by a short, black man. Kilkirk.

"What the fuck? How are you alive?"

"I'm immortal, lads!" he said with a maniacal laugh.

"Yes, I just drink his blood because immortal blood is the best kind, you know?" said Kesimir.

"So, Kilkirk really is a leprechaun?" Bark asked.

"Fuck no, dickface!" said Clint. "Look at him. He's a god-damn djinn, you know, like a genie. We found him in North Africa trapped in a brazier. We made him give us a wish in order for us to release him. And we wished that he would always dress and act like a leprechaun! Isn't that the awesomest wish ever?"

"So what the hell is all this about?" demanded Bark.

"Dude," said Leon. "We were just fucking with you. Hazing, dork!"

"Good times!" howled Kesimir.

"We can leave then?" Bark said.

"If you want to, sure, go ahead," said Sooter with a dismissive wave.

"Wait. Can I still have sex with the girl?" asked Drip nervously.

"Oky-doky," Ichigo said. "Just go in butt cause I don't like baby."

"Instant boner," said Drip, wide-eyed.

"I think I'll go wait in the car," said Bark.

"If that's how you want to play it, little dude. The rest of us are gonna jerk off while your friend pounds out Ichigo. Her butthole is like a steel trap."

"It was very nice meeting you, Bark," said Sooter with an unnatural leer. The old man stood in an effeminate pose, index finger pressed to his lip. "I hope you don't hold our shenanigans against us too much. Please, feel free to come back any time."

As Bark walked down the corridor, he could hear Sooter scolding the others, "Don't waste! Be sure to save your cock sauce in a cup for me. I've worked up quite a thirst tonight, boys."

Bark could not stop thinking about what a stupid night it was to have forgotten his magical sword at home. It would really come in handy on nights like this, when mystery rules and evil goofs off.

DEAD BUG DETECTIVE

She was all legs. She strolled into my office like she was walking up a waterspout. Tap dancing her way into my pants. But that would have to wait.

"You're the detective?" she asked, incredulously.

"Yeah, doll. I'm him."

"The dead bug detective?"

"In the flesh," I said and kicked back. Took a swig of bourbon.

"Do you remember everything I told you on the phone?"

"I got a memory like a steel trap. Full of feet."

"Then," she said, "you'll take my case?"

"Oke," I said, setting my highball glass on my desk and reaching my hand out in hopes she would pay me in cash.

"I'm afraid I have no money right now," she said, looking away like a bashful lamb at its mother's execution.

"I'm sure you can work something out," I encouraged.

She spread her legs, all zillion of them. Some millipedes are just giving it away.

But I had no time for that. I'm a dead bug detective.

———◦◦◦———

If I could pay my bills in insect vagina, I'd be set. I had a portfolio full of boudoir snapshots that would make a cellar stairwell slug blush. When you are in the dead bug biz, sex follows you like stink on a dying dog. Satan was constantly ringing me up for one look at my stag beetle reels. Not the real Satan—the robot that the Church built so that they'd have a physical representation of evil to shake their fists at while flagellating themselves. Robot Satan was one sick bird. No kind of medicine cures his ill.

I know what you're thinking—millipedes aren't insects. They're diplopods. Insects have six legs. Yeah, you are right. But have you seen a millipede pussy? Put a photo of one right next to a mantis pussy—you seriously cannot tell the difference. Come to that, arachnids, chilopods, pantopods, horseshoe crabs, and crustaceans all got that same damn pussy.

Fossilized trilobites got that same pussy.

And you are also thinking robots don't take medicine. Well, there's where you are wrong. They got special electro-tronic capsules full of, like, microchips or nanobots that they take when they get buggy or glitchy or whatever the hell the kids are calling it these days.

But I had work to do. I'm a dead bug detective.

———◦———

The place looked like it was hit in the Blitz. Holes in the ceiling big enough to climb a beanstalk through. Pieces of rubble the size of small children. And the stink—that mildewed stink.

"He's usually about, just around nightfall," the woman said. She looked like she hadn't seen the inside of a functional bathroom since before there were 48 states. Like she had no idea what running water was. "He glows, you know."

"Yeah, I've heard that about spirits," I told her. I lit up a butt and puffed it hard. "You sure he knows where that key is?"

"Not sure, but there's a good chance. It fell down into the floorboards. And that's where he spent most of his life."

"Yeah, that sounds like a good bet," I said and offered her a drag from my cig. She declined but eyed it jealously.

Then I saw some scurrying motion at the edge of the baseboard. A ghostly aura made it more obvious than it might have been otherwise. The spirit of a little boy cockroach. He crawled across the floor and did a solemn jig. Silently. Ghosts don't tap dance.

"Hey there, little fella," I said to him, tossing a morsel of food down in front of him. One thing cockroaches like, it's something to nibble on. Gets them talking every damn time.

The kid sniffed the bit of sausage with his little feelers.

"He might think it's poison," the woman whispered. "That's what got him."

"It's okay, buddy. Not poison," I told him, though it wouldn't have mattered none of it was poison or not to his ghost metabolism.

After some moments of reluctant pussyfooting, the tyke bit right into the scrap and gobbled it gone.

"Yeah, that's right," I said approvingly. "Now, buddy, have you seen a key? A little shiny, gold key?"

He looked at me with his dead bug eyes. Bug eyes all look dead, but dead bugs eyes are extra dead. He gazed double-dead eyed at me. Like he didn't understand a word I was saying to him.

"If you know where the key is, why dontcha be a good lad and show me to it?"

Still nothing. No sign of intellect in his eyes. But in a flash, he turned and walked over to a place where the floor was rough. He stood next to a floorboard that was buckled, eyeing it repeatedly.

I pried the edge of the board up, just enough to see the glint of a key.

"Thanks, buddy," I said and gave him another bit of sausage.

"Can you help him?" the woman asked me. "Can you show him to the other side or something?"

"Lady, I got no time for that." I snatched up the key. "I'm a dead bug detective."

———————◄O►———————

The inside of the coffin was bringing me down. They could have sprung for nicer digs, but instead I was sealed up in a plain pine box with felt lining, like a case you might keep some croquet mallets in. I understood the scrimping. I wasn't going to be in here very long. I was just dying to get undead.

A few more seconds and Jag would be here to dig me up.

A few more seconds, and I was still waiting. I clicked my mandibles nervously and scratched at the lid with all six of my extremities. It's like I woke up this way and I was late for work.

"Get me the hell out of here!" I roared like a caged tiger. I could feel the air running out. Could Jag have sold me out for some millipede pussy? For favor with the Silverfish gang?

I didn't have time to find out.

I couldn't wait one more second.

I'm a dead bug detective.

THE BALANCING ACT

Everett Carnes, while balancing his checkbook, discovered quite by accident that he had a very good sense of balance. That's when he decided to become a tightrope walker. Though he had lived all fifty-seven years of his life walking on solid ground, and occasionally on boats, he did not fear making the transition, despite the urgings of his family and closest friends. He was looking over a brochure for a tightrope walking school one evening as he visited his elderly father in the old man's downtown apartment.

His father shook with palsy and trembled so dreadfully that it impeded his speech, and as such, the old man barely ever spoke except to ask for food or cigarettes or pin-ups of sumptuous blondes. But on this day, while jerking his spoon around in a bowl of yellowish porridge, the old man managed to stammer, "You can't go to that school. They don't let in heathens."

Everett, quite taken aback by this sudden and atypical insult, tossed down the brochure and, with steely eyes, stared at the old man. "What on earth do you mean, Father?"

Licking away some porridge that had clung to his bottom lip, the old man shrugged his tremulous shoulders. "On your mother's side," he finally said. Then, having found the spoon too difficult to control, he stuck his face right into the dish and began to slurp the porridge like a starved swine.

His son couldn't grasp what the old man meant. "I'm sorry, Father, but what do you mean when you say *heathen*? And don't suck up your gruel like that. It is quite off-putting."

The wrinkled old face, smeared with yellow, grinned toothlessly at Everett. "It's a long story, and my memory is not so good. Wrap me up in a papoose and carry me about with you wherever you go. I will tell you what I can recall as I recall it."

Everett's mother had been dead for fifteen years, and he did not keep in close contact with any of the surviving relatives on her side. The family seemed decent, conformist folk with solid, orthodox traditions. The possibility that they could be of a heathen line was alarming to Everett, who had only read about such people in pulp novels that he had stolen as a youth from gas stations while on vacation in the South.

Fixing up a papoose for his father proved only slightly more difficult than he had imagined. The old man was afflicted with a wasting disease that had shrunken him to roughly the size of a two-year-old. If the old man hadn't been rocking about with palsy, then Everett would have had no trouble at all. Everett walked down the narrow alley adjacent to the apartment building with his father strapped firmly to his chest. The old man began hooting like an owl, the sound echoing off the brick walls and all around the alley. "Does that ring any bells?" he asked when he was done whooping.

"What will it do to my reputation as a tightrope walker to be seen with my father hooting at this time of evening? Should I claim he is my pet hoot-owl to save further embarrassment?" Everett snarled.

His father slapped his face. "At a time like this! Why do you think only of yourself, and of aspects of yourself that only apply in the imagination, I might add? You are too old to entertain such fanciful notions. I would like you to take me on a trip so that I can relax and think of all that I can remember. Let us voyage far away to an exotic locale full of good food, fine cigarettes, and sumptuous brunettes."

A woman wearing a headscarf and a long skirt approached.

"Oh, isn't he a little fellow!" she said, looking at Everett's father. "I will pinch your cheek!" she threatened playfully, though she didn't actually pinch him at all. "Is he yours?" she asked Everett.

Everett didn't quite know what to say. "Yes... he's my father, if that's what you mean."

The woman looked at him with lowered brow.

"Is that meant to be a joke?"

"No, I'm quite serious, madam."

"This is a baby, not more than two years of age. Anyone can tell as much!"

"He's my father, shrunken from a wasting disease and nigh eighty years old, I assure you."

She gave out a loud raspberry, and then played peek-a-boo with his father, whom it delighted a great deal. This made Everett wonder if he was mistaken. It was possible, he concluded, that he had somehow grabbed a baby instead of his father, in which case he must hurry back up to the apartment before his father became too angry with him for mistaking him for an infant. The lady glared at Everett, kissed the baby or his father, and then moved along. Everett turned around, heading back to his father's rooms.

When back in the apartment, Everett called out, "Father! Are you here?" He was now quite sure that he had a baby strapped to his chest. "I'm sorry I left you behind, Father. It's only that I didn't realize there was a baby around here."

"What is that you say, Son?" asked a voice behind him.

Turning, all he saw was his father's small terrier dog, standing on its hind legs. "Why do you stand so, on your back legs? Isn't it uncomfortable for you?"

"What a question to ask one's father!" the dog replied, but Everett was not really sure that this was his father's dog at all. For one thing, his father's dog did not speak so far as he knew, and his father's dog did not have hands or a mustache but was covered in quite a bit more hair. No, he concluded, this must be his naked, aged father. His father never had a dog, he recalled.

"Who is this baby I have strapped to my chest?" Everett said.

"Why would you ask me? I am but an old man, living alone and naked for want of a better wardrobe. Is he one of your mother's heathen clan? Have they spread their seed the earth over, even into my own rooms that I would prefer to keep private and free from all babies? Why would they do such a thing, I wonder?"

"I wonder the same myself," Everett said, and then began to unstrap the little tyke from his breast.

"What are you doing?" asked the baby. "Are you letting this circus dog confuse you because you dream of being a tightrope walker? Clearly, someone has trained this dog to walk on its hind legs, to shave but for its mustache, and to pretend to be your father. Any circus midget could pull off such a feat, I suspect."

"Who are you, baby?" Everett asked him.

"Who do you say that I am?"

Everett's thoughts were swirling in his head in the manner he imagined hashish-eaters' thoughts might. He could not make sense of the situation at all. He knew he needed his father for something, and since he couldn't be sure which of these was his father, he took the baby under one arm and the dog under the other and set off for his home, where he believed himself to be headed before the confusion began.

The streets were empty of carriages and cabs, and the night was quiet but for the faint rustle of leaves when the light breeze gathered in the limbs of the few trees there in the city. "What was it I wanted to know?" Everett wondered aloud.

"You wanted to know which one of us is your father," said the babe-father.

"You wanted to know why spies would be infiltrating my home," said the dog-father.

"You wanted to know the seven secrets of my recipe for gruel."

"You wanted to know the weight of the sky."

"You wanted to know the meaning of the word 'word.'"

"You once asked me where babies come from," said the dog-father.

"You also asked me why the dog humped your leg," said the babe-father.

Everett stopped walking and looked first at the dog-father, then at the babe-father. "I'm sure all those questions needed answering, although I can't help but feel that I had another question in mind tonight. Didn't you say something to me that caused me to question the nature of my own existence?" Before him, the street narrowed, becoming a sort of bridge—or rather more of a gangplank—over a deep ravine. "I'm certain this is the way home, but I don't recall a ravine. They must be doing road construction."

He pulled a long, mostly straight limb from one of the trees that lined the path, and tied the dog to one end, the babe to the other. He approached the plank cautiously, as was his wont, holding the limb at the middle and using the weight of each of his fathers as counterbalances. "Don't squirm around, Fathers, or we will fall into the ravine."

"If you are really my son, you'll run across this plank as if it were a four-lane bridge! You'll fly as you've never flown before, for I tire of being bound to this tree limb," the babe-father screeched.

"If you are really *my* son, and half heathen also, then you should hop! Hop all the way across this plank, as though you are a demented rabbit on its way to lay decorative eggs, for that is how a true heathen behaves given the opportunity," the dog-father barked.

"Your requests seem far too dangerous. Perhaps also a bit nonsensical. Both of you, quiet yourselves so that I may concentrate my efforts." Everett took a small step forward. The plank sagged and bounced slightly as he shifted his weight. Looking across the expanse, the narrow walkway seemed much longer and the ravine much wider than they had seemed to Everett before. He inched his way slowly but artfully toward the center of the plank, using his fathers to steady himself.

"You must go halfway before you can reach your destination," he told himself. And when he reached the center, he stopped. "I could really use a drink."

Something glittery approached from the opposite side of the plank.

"What is it? What can it be? A mekanik, man of metal and gadgetry? Who else could be so shiny and daring?" speculated the babe-father.

"I think it is perhaps one of the stars' children. A fallen space angel that is forced to patrol planks and smite heathens. Beware, my son!" warned the dog-father.

As the figure drew closer, Everett realized it was simply a cocktail waitress. She winked at him, heaved her bosom, and offered him a martini-cocktail from a tray.

Everett pursed his lips and furrowed his brow. "I fear that I'll lose my balance if I take the drink. Thank you anyway."

"If you ask me," said the cocktail waitress, "you have already lost it. You're suspended hundreds of feet in the air with a dog and a baby tied to a branch." She then huffed, turned abruptly, and missed her footing. Everett lost sight of her in the darkness of the chasm long before he heard her hit the ground.

"Congratulations, Son, you've passed the first test!" said the baby.

"Yes, the temptation of a busty beauty offering you alcohol could have spelled your demise. You are well on your way to completing your quest!" said the dog.

"I have a quest?"

"Like all heathens before you, you seek to attain salvation via a physical idol or fetish," said the dog, who then proceeded to bark unintelligible directives into the night sky.

"You are questing after the entrance into a school building that appears entirely sealed off from the exterior," cooed the baby, who gurgled and then suggested: "Perhaps there is a subterranean tunnel."

Throughout the broken conversation, Everett impelled himself steadily forward, always carefully but with an air of comfort and ease. The board creaked and squeaked as his fathers continuously harangued him, yet he did not lose his composure. He could see that the end of the plank was now in sight. There was a blinding spotlight in his eyes, he noticed.

"That must be why it was so hard to make out who the waitress was."

"You should have known it was the waitress," said the dog.

"Yes, you asked her for a drink," said the baby.

"And then you didn't even take the drink."

"And then you watched her die without even tipping her."

"Leave me alone!" Everett cried. "Just a few more feet now!"

He made it across safely. There was the obligatory step near the end where he nearly slipped, taking the three of them to their deaths below, and just at the last second regained balance, but it would have been melodramatic and predictable to highlight that small part of the journey, so it is noted only in retrospect.

As soon as he set his foot onto solid ground, a raucous round of applause went up. He stared into the blinding light, visibly shaken for the first time that night. Tables, wine glasses, diners: He was home, he realized. Everyone was having dinner, and he was the show. Apparently, he was a hit. Setting the limb down, he took a bow and a little girl skated over to hand him a bouquet of lilies.

He found his family seated near the back, clapping unenthusiastically and hiding in shadows. After untying the dog, who wandered off in search of table scraps, and untying the baby, whom he handed to the closest wet nurse, Everett made his way to the table where his brothers and sisters sat. They were all there, all nineteen of them, from his youngest brother Petry, aged 10, to his eldest sister Pertelope, aged 67.

Everett took one of the empty seats and, smiling, asked everyone, "Well, what did you think?" He was greeted by twenty grimaces. He recounted. Yes, there were twenty guests at this table. The twentieth was a woman of great age, wearing a gown the color of dust. In fact, her whole aspect gave the impression of cobweb and mustiness. "Mother?" Everett said in a weak voice.

"Your antics woke her, you fool," Paoli scolded, wagging a baby carrot at Everett.

"Your hijinks nearly destroyed the family," added Peg, with a tilt of the flask.

"With Mother awake, I can't have any dessert!" Praetor ranted, who had been watching his weight unsuccessfully since early adolescence.

"Silence," rasped the dry, dying-moth voice of Mother. "All of you, silence! I want to tell Everett what I thought of his act."

Everett leaned forward in anticipation. Mother smiled, coughed out a ball of lint, and shrilled: "A little more wine would be nice!"

Patriciana whispered in his ear, "Pinky tells me that you are thinking of becoming a tightrope walker. What's that all about? You are over fifty, and look at you! Losing your hair *and* you wear glasses. Not exactly the image of the circus man that most children have in their minds."

Everett stood and proclaimed, "All of you, listen to me now. I've just come across a two hundred yard plank, suspended hundreds of feet in the air, holding one or more of our fathers, and I did it all without the safeguard of a net. I would appreciate it if you ceased implying I'm insane for thinking I can walk a tight rope as a career!"

After some gasps and chokes, his family looked back at him in a way that implied he was insane. "I hope you don't think that your little stunt qualifies you for consideration as an applicant at the tightrope walking school," Pippy said. "They specifically state that they walk tightropes only. It's not plank-walking school, for crying out loud!"

"Any common pirate can walk a plank. Any laborer!" Patmos added.

"Any man about to die," said the dog-father who was being fed shreds of chicken under the table by Mother.

Mother pursed her cracked lips. "I'm surprised you thought this was your father. Father's been dead for 150 years, dearling. We didn't have the heart to tell you because we know you've always been so sensitive. This is just a stray dog from the Isle of Man, of the kind which are known to make noises that can be mistaken, from a certain distance, for human speech."

"Like the legendary leucrota," the dog added.

"Quite right," Mother agreed.

"And the peryton, for which I am named," said Peryton, "is known to cast a shadow that appears to be a man, though his physical form is a bird with the head of a stag."

Everett regarded his own shadow, a long one as the spotlight was still trained on him. It was hard to tell if this was the shadow of a man or boy, a fool or a king.

"Well, what about the baby?" Everett said.

"What *about* the baby?" Mother retorted. "Probably grow up to be a scoundrel on the dole. Or else he'll invent a pill that makes children so confident at school that they never need to cry. A ne'er-do-well. A reprobate. Couldn't you see it in his gaze?"

"I saw my father in his gaze, but only when I didn't see a baby."

"Your father *was* a baby. He died at birth. Had to stuff him and keep him on the back of a shelf in the closet so he wouldn't scare the children."

Everett shuddered and drew away in horror. "I don't like where this conversation is headed. Brothers, sisters... good day to you all."

He headed to his bedroom, but he forgot that his corridor was being repaired and currently had no floor. Fishing a cable from his pocket, he made a lasso and managed to snag it on the banister. Once he had staked the other end to the edge of the remaining flooring, he removed his shoes and placed one in each pocket. Then stepped out onto the cable, which he made sure was pulled quite tight indeed.

"I don't know who he's trying to impress," said his siblings while he inched along, several feet in the air. They finished their shrimp cocktails and went home.

Upstairs, Everett was alone. Truly alone for the first time he could recall. It was not quite the prison he'd always feared it would be. He actually felt quite confident, in the defiant manner of those who are more comfortable ignoring the reality thrust upon them from the outside. But as he removed his cravat, he couldn't help but feel as though there was one last thing he needed to do. A confrontation. He couldn't have had it out with the indomitable horde of his siblings, and his mother was probably too fragile, having just returned from the grave, to handle his explosion. There was the one, though. The one person he really needed to give a piece of his mind.

He removed his hard-soled leather shoes and put on his soft slippers in hopes this would allow him to make a sneaky approach. The slippers did not disappoint. The junk closet never heard him coming.

He flung open the door, catching the dust goblins completely off guard. Grabbing the largest of the fuzzy, spider-legged creatures, he shouted, "Bring me my father!" Spittle showered the ugly thing as it cowered and tried to shield itself with stick-like arms too thin to provide any weather protection. "Summon him from whatever dank cranny of gloom he's ensconced himself in, you foul collections of sloughed scree!" he commanded the others. They skittered and skirred into various nooks between faded Whosit? and Boggle boxes, betwixt unstrung racquets and deflated pigskins, under the globe that was off its spindle and over old bits of glued-together seashells, driftwood, and burlap. He sneered at the goblin in his hand, showing his teeth, then released it several inches from the floor, precipitating a frightening tumble to the floor before it dazedly gathered its wits and scrambled behind a grimy pair of galoshes.

Everett closed the closet door and pressed his ear to it for a listen. It was quiet for almost a minute. Then he could make out a few soft taps, the scooting of boxes, and a clank or two. Then silence again.

When Everett reopened the closet, his father was there on the top shelf. His feet were stapled to a wedge of plywood, a short length of 2X2 tacked to his back for support. He was clothed in the shabby skins of a caveman doll, and someone had put a dog-hair wig on his cue ball head as a sort of joke. All over his long-dead newborn body was soot. They had smoked him to preserve him. This seemed fitting to Everett. His father loved to smoke. Brittle, charred skin cracked away around the mouth, revealing pearly teeth. Could his father have been born with teeth? That was supposedly lucky—for the infant but not the mother.

"Father," said Everett, suddenly unsure of what he could say.

Everett reached up and took his stuffed father in his hands. His father was much lighter than he expected.

"Father, I'm sorry you were preserved in this heathen fashion. But I am also glad to have the chance to tell you that I'm done with being a son. I'd like to give you a proper burial, but I have no yard. You'll have to settle for this."

He took his father down the stairs and stared at the hole in the torn-up floor. "I'm going to start a new family all my own," he said to his father, "hundreds of feet off the ground. A sky family. A perfect family with perfect balance. Heads in the clouds, feet on a rope. I think things might have come out differently for me if only you'd let me become a pilot instead of giving me the genes for legal blindness."

The cracked maw seemed to mock the wishful ropewalker.

Everett huffed, dropping the pitiful husk of his sire into the hole. He exploded on impact, engulfing his son in flame.

Redness.

Blackness.

Whiteness.

The only way to travel between the clouds in Heaven, Everett found, was by tightrope.

THE BOYS IN A BOX

I. Herman Stage meets Michale Horns

Herman Stage kept the boys in a box, mainly because the refrigerator was too small, and a wet sack didn't provide sufficient protection from the meat crabs who always managed to find a way inside his hovel. He filled the box with cool, damp leaves and left it in the root cellar. He wanted to age the boys. They were young and tender and still needed a little time.

As he tromped up the stone stairs, he crushed two meat crabs, their innards shooting forth like graying pus from a lanced boil. The crunching sound made him flinch despite his hatred for the creatures. He'd lost more meals to these vermin than he cared to tally, which made these events a rare exception; he kept a note pad with him to keep track of how many times he sneezed, yawned, scratched an itch, defecated, ate, saw an oddly shaped yam, burped, or vomited in any given day. At fifty-six, his list of tallies had grown exceptionally long. He no longer bothered to update his database weekly. Too much of his time was spent finding ways to trick or kill the crabs. Fire was one of the least effective ways to kill them, but he found that if he dug a deep trench along the perimeter of his property and filled it with flaming oil, the crabs would generally not cross over onto his land as long as the fires blazed. Getting enough oil was a problem.

At first, he had resorted to robbing his neighbors, the closest of which was over five miles distant, of engine oil. This substance was easiest to get to because they keep their trucks and farm vehicles outdoors. It was only weeks later when he decided to burglarize kitchens for cooking oils. He needed more neighbors, or they needed to buy more oil because the trench was nearly impossible to keep filled. He had resorted to rendering fats of animals himself in a makeshift lab in one of his old barns.

Another issue proved to be finding a path across his blazing moat off his land in search of more oil. He built a bridge of steel-reinforced concrete, but it got hot enough to melt the tires of his old Studebaker, so he started taking his father's mechanical spider everywhere. It stood about twelve feet high, made of black metal. The ride was not smooth, but as he sat in the cockpit of the robotic monstrosity, he certainly felt a lot more menacing than he did behind the wheel of an antique truck. The spider was black, the Studebaker green. The spider walked its way over the moat. No bridge needed.

The only problem with the mechanical spider was that its joints were notoriously delicate and required a great deal of lubrication, which meant he needed even more oil. It also ran on a peculiar fuel, one that was not easy to come by. His father had never made it clear to him why he had designed it in such a questionable way. He had only made it clear that the vehicle ran on the blood of hobbledehoys: males at the exact point when boyhood ends and manhood is about to begin. Any other blood was likely to clog the engine permanently. The fuel tank also held only 20 pints at a time. This is why the two boys were in the box. They needed to age a little, to cease to be boys. The box was meant to retard the progress of their becoming full-blown men, to give him time to drain their blood which he could not fit in the spider at this point in time.

Trouble arrived one afternoon in the form of a traveling magician who had disguised himself as a talking fox, which was the style at the time. This fox was called Michale Horns, and all his promotional posters showed horns atop his vulpine head. Many a bright-eyed show-goer was disappointed to find out that he had no horns at all, not even when he was disguised as a fox, and it wasn't uncommon for his trailer to be set ablaze as a result. This had led Michale Horns to handcraft all his own sets and equipment from fireproof materials. His cape, for instance, would not burn. He made shoes to fit his little fox feet, and these shoes were also heat resistant. When he happened upon the blazing moat, it was nothing for him to cross it using his wits and flameproof kit.

Herman Stage, who had never liked magicians even at age eight, immediately clambered out of his spider, for he had been ready to go out on an oil raid and prepared to give the fox magician a hearty dose of what-for. But before he could even speak the words "Get off my land, you no good, skin-changing rascal!" Michale Horns had set up for a brilliant stage show and invited every meat crab within a thirty-mile radius. Even the two boys climbed out of the box, but they did so in slow motion because all those chill, moist leaves had made them sluggish.

But finally, Herman Stage did manage to utter the phrase: "Get off my land, you no good, skin-changing rascal!"

The fox magician looked at him hungrily.

"I'd have to give all these crabs and people their money back, and I can barely afford to eat as it is! Can't you see how hungry I am?"

He looked famished, but Herman Stage was still not convinced. He pulled his hambremeter from his pocket and measured the fox magician's hunger level. The reading was through the roof, so Herman Stage gave the fox magician three pieces of candy that were in his pocket at the time for just such a situation. The fox scarfed them down without even taking off the wrappers.

"What else you got?"

"Only odds and ends," said Herman Stage. "I can let you have the ears and noses of the two boys, 'cause there's not much blood in there. You can have all the silage you can swallow, but it's old and smells like mildew. You can eat the meat crabs, too, for all I care about them. But for the sake of Cripes, don't do this stage show on my land. I have oil to steal and animals to render!" He pulled the notepad from his pocket and marked a tally on the page labeled "Tell Stranger Not to Have Stage Show on Land." This page was relatively barren, with only two score marks visible.

The fox magician was very clever.

"Can I tell you a story?" he asked. "Because if I can, then I will."

"How do I know that if I say you can tell me a story, you will actually tell me a story?" Herman Stage's challenge was spoken in a cold tone, one which said that he'd been burned before on storytelling deals.

The fox magician handed him a lump of fool's gold.

"Here, you can keep this until I have told you one complete story." He proceeded to tell a story, but I'm not going to write it as he told it because he made it longer than it needed to be. This is how I would tell it:

"There was a boy named Dylan Wirch who was not very bright but managed to get himself a girlfriend nonetheless. She lived in Virginia, he in Maryland. In the beginning, they talked together online and texted at first. But he wanted so badly to be with her in real life that he decided to hitchhike hundreds of miles to hold her in his arms. He packed himself some crusts of bread and rib bones that were nearly picked clean, tying them up in a handkerchief on the end of a stick. Dylan set out to make his way in the world. But first, he met on his path a small fox who told him to beware of strangers who would give him rides.

"'Dylan Wirch,' said the small fox, 'all you will ever need is in your bag on the end of your stick.'

"And then the fox was hit by a car. The car stopped. The driver got out and took a long look at the bleeding fox. Then he walked over to Dylan and said, 'Hi, my boy. Do you need a lift?'

"'Yes,' said Dylan Wirch. 'My name is Dylan Wirch, and I'm heading down to Virginia to meet my girlfriend for the first time.'

"'Oh, good!' said the man. 'I'm her father. I'll take you right to her house. She's very excited to meet you, Dylan.'

"'You are Tanya's dad? I can't believe my luck!' Dylan tossed his stick and sack into some roadside bushes. 'Guess I won't be needing those anymore.' And he got in the car with the man and they drove off and sang children's campfire songs together for about an hour. Then the man pulled the car into a very spooky driveway of a rundown house.

"'We're here. Welcome to Virginia, Dylan." The man grinned. His teeth were large and horse-like. His breath smelled like criminal insanity. But Dylan remained oblivious to any signs of danger. He even overlooked the red and black 'Danger!' sign posted in the man's front yard.

"'Come on inside with me, my boy, and I'll show you to Tanya's room.'

"'Is she as pretty in real life as she is my imagination?'

"'You'll know in one hot minute, now won't you?' The two exited the car and entered the rundown old house. It seemed the floor was carpeted with beer bottles and the walls painted with nicotine. But Dylan was still not concerned. All he could think about was boobs and the fact that Tanya had them. When they got to a small, dingy bedroom, the man grabbed Dylan and handcuffed his wrists together behind his back.

"'Now we are going to have some real fun,' said the man as he threw Dylan to the floor.

"'Tanya will be so ashamed that her dad is acting like this. Stop, mister! Think of your daughter.'

"The man just looked at Dylan as if he now realized this kid was truly a moron. I mean, there had been clues, but the man wasn't too bright himself. He leaned over and started unbuckling Dylan's belt. Before the young lad knew it, the man had stripped away his pants. Then Dylan found himself flipped around on his belly with his face eating ashy carpet. But luck was still on young Dylan's side, it would seem, because earlier there had not been enough room in the makeshift travel bag upon a stick to stow his bottle of lemon-lime drink and his Skittles candies. The only other place he could think to put them was in his rectum. You know, for safekeeping. So when the man went to violate Dylan, he was unsuccessful, the sudden emergence of loose, assorted fruit candies catching him so off guard that he fell and impaled himself on a spear that he really shouldn't have left lying around in his bedroom."

"Was there supposed to be a moral to that story?" Herman Stage asked the fox magician.

"I'm sure there was, but I don't have time to explain it to you. I'm way too hungry for that. Anyhow, I've got a show to do. Give me back my iron pyrite."

II. The Boys in a Box

The boys became warmer as they sat and waited for the show to begin. They'd been thoroughly chilled in the box. Now their metabolisms began to speed up and their thoughts to quicken. Suddenly, they realized they were free to go. Herman Stage was distracted.

"Let's get out of here," said Martin, the slightly older, slightly better-looking boy.

"We can take the spider," said Randy, eyes brightening.

"Do you know how to drive a mechanical spider?"

"How hard can it be?"

"Probably harder than a car, wouldn't you say?"

"I don't know. I can't drive a car," said Randy. He snuck over to the arachnoid vehicle. Martin followed.

The two squeezed into the hatch, barely able to fit in the cockpit. Randy turned a key left conveniently in the ignition switch. A purring sound came from the underbelly.

"I think I started it," he said. He grabbed at some levers in front of him, and the cockpit shifted and jerked as the legs moved.

"We're walking," Martin said.

"Yes indeed! Let's book it on out of here!" Randy pressed on a pedal that may or may not have made them go faster. They looked out the small portholes that served as spider-eyes and saw the spider legs crushing dozens of meat crabs, but they didn't feel bad because the meat crabs would have gladly devoured them.

"Almost to the moat," Randy said. "Then we are home free."

"Really?"

"'Really' what?"

"You make it sound like you know exactly what we are going to do now that we've escaped."

"Anything we want," Randy said playfully. "We are hobbledehoys. No longer boys, not quite men."

"We'll have to ditch the spider pretty soon," Martin said. "The fuel gauge is practically on *S*."

"What do you mean?"

"The gauge spells out SPIDER, and I'm pretty sure that when the needle goes to S, it's empty."

"I see a barn up ahead. We can ditch there."

They hid the spider behind the barn, clambered out, and proceeded toward a farmhouse. As they closed in on it, they saw what looked like a party going on. Lots of young children, much younger than either of them, were running around in cowboy hats. Several vendors operated stands.

"Step right up!" called a woman dressed like Calamity Jane. "Point a real gun at someone! Only five dollars!"

They walked over to her little booth. An array of pistols and shotguns were laid out on a picnic table.

"You are letting these little kids point guns at people?" Martin said.

"For five dollars, I surely am," she said.

A towheaded boy of no more than five, shirtless and in cowboy boots, handed the woman a five-dollar bill smeared with what they hoped was chocolate.

"Which'un?" the woman asked.

"That'un," the little kid said, pointing to a Colt pocket pistol.

She handed it over and said, "Remember to point it directly at the person and aim for the mass of their body, not a limb or the head."

He pointed the gun right at Randy.

"That's not loaded, right?" Randy asked the woman.

"Huh?" she said, looking up from a hunting magazine. "Shouldn't be."

"You didn't check?" Martin shouted.

"There are over a dozen different firearms here, boys. I can't know what is going on with every one of them at all times. I'm not a damn gun wizard."

The blond kid held the gun pointed straight at Randy's chest, squinting one eye.

"I'm pointing this gun at you!" the kid yelled.

"Yeah, I know! Stop it!" Randy said.

"No way. I paid five bucks to point this gun at you, and I'm going to point it real hard!"

Randy looked back at the woman who ran the booth. "Is there some kind of time limit for how long he gets the gun?"

"Technically, yep," she said. "But since there ain't a line right now, I'm fine with letting him just point it to his heart's content."

"I'm afraid he's pointing it at my heart's content," Randy said.

"You know," Martin said, "we can just walk away, right?"

And they walked away. The towheaded kid kept Randy in his sights until they made it to the next stall, then turned it on the woman.

A canvas tent big enough to hold about a dozen people had a sign above the entrance that read "Radical Theories in

Modern Psychology." The boys ducked inside. It was dimly lit. A man behind a podium was speaking to empty seats.

"And the notion of a kitten crushed beneath the millstone, or the compression of the puppy skull, such that the eyes are ejected from their orbits by spurting brain matter, are anathema to the human mind. How is it that the kitten and the puppy are both constructed so effectively to stimulate human empathic response? Would the notion extend to fox kit? Note that the fox, although canine, is given the feline name for its offspring. The fox is, no doubt, the most feline of all canines. The most canine of all felines is, as we all know, the cheetah. Could I hit a cheetah with a speeding car to elicit sympathy from the minds of men? Surely at top speed, a cheetah would stand no chance of outrunning my Stingray. Is it worth it, for the sake of demonstration? Blood on the bumper? Potential body damage? But it would drive home, no pun intended, the point that mankind will hit any animal with a car given a long enough time frame. The look on a kitten's face is still interpreted as portraying human emotion. The quizzical head-cocking of puppies still indicates to our mind human thought. But, allow me to demonstrate," he said, pulling a tarp from a table with several puppies and kittens tied down to it.

The two slipped out quickly and marched toward the house, desperate to escape the previous scene.

Randy spotted a girl about their age sitting at a picnic table and eating an ice cream cone. She had all the hallmarks of an attractive female, including whatever hairstyle was currently in fashion and the type of glasses the hip kids wore.

"Oh. My. God," he said.

"What?" Martin asked.

"I think I'm in love with that girl."

"The one seductively licking that vanilla cone?"

"That would be the one."

"We should go over so you can meet her."

She saw them approaching and smiled.

"Hi, guys," she said.

"I hate your dad," Randy said.

"What? How do you even know who my dad is?" she asked with a scoff.

"Randy's just a little awkward," Martin said, rushing to his friend's defense. "He means 'hello.'"

"Yeah, hello," Randy said dazedly.

"So, you guys new here?" she said. She licked the ice cream lusciously, not making eye contact with either of them.

"Why do you ask?" Martin said.

"Don't know. I have a hard time telling who is new and who is old."

"My name is Randy," Randy said.

"Yeah, your friend already said that. My name is Zargothni."

"That's a funny name. My name is Martin."

Zargothni burst out laughing. "Martin? That's like a name out of a comic book about nerds too boring to exist."

"Martin is the name of a wooden donkey lawn ornament that basically raised me once my parents succumbed to tennis. I named myself after it."

"Well, I hope I didn't offend you," she said dryly. "Orphans can be... touchy."

"My name is Randy," Randy said again, reaching out to touch her hair.

"Uh... excuse me, Randy. You have to wash your filthy hands before touching my stylish hair."

Randy awkwardly withdrew his hand, turning his gaze to his shoes.

"You see, Zargothni, Randy, and I have been kept in a box by a strange man who planned to use our blood to fuel his giant walking spider. So Randy's a little awkward around anyone who isn't a meat crab."

"Okay. I see. When you said you hated my dad, I thought you must have seen *The Two Men Who Kept Hugging*."

The boys shook their heads.

"My dad is Cam Davies. He's a liberal."

The boys stared blankly.

"It means he likes to kiss boys and hug trees. He made a movie, *The Two Men Who Kept Hugging*, and it won some awards. But also, a lot of people want to kill him now because the two men in the movie get stuck in a cave with nothing but a Bible, so they end up using the pages to wipe their butts. Plus, they keep hugging, and a lot of folks think that's not normal. Even a lot of men who keep hugging other men think that the hugging shown in that film was unnatural. So, it would make perfect sense if you hated my dad."

"Do you hate him?" Martin asked.

"Of course. He's my dad."

"From what I remember about my dad," Randy said, "I think I feared him, and I loved him, and he made me mad and sad, but I don't remember ever hating him."

"Well," she said with a shrug, "that's your loss."

"It's probably a pretty big part of his identity," Martin said firmly. "And as far as I know, I don't hate my dad either. It's not a freaking badge of honor."

"Never said it was," she said, flicking her hair back.

"Hey," Randy said, suddenly lucid. "What's going on here anyhow?"

"It's Blue Beaver Creek's annual Dolphin Days," she said. "So, I take it that means you guys are new here."

"Yes, we are new," Martin said. "What's Dolphin Days?"

"The mayor of Blue Beaver Creek is scared of sharks, so every Shark Week he holds a big celebration called Dolphin Days, and no one is allowed to watch TV, but we have all kinds of events, like this."

Randy looked around. "I don't see any dolphins."

"Yeah," she said with a sigh, "they are pretty expensive and not much fun. The males tried to rape one of the volunteers a few years back. So now there is just one guy, my stupid brother, who goes around in a cheap, smelly dolphin suit. Other than that, it's just a big carnival-slash-Bible-school-slash-haunted-hayride."

"I guess that's pretty cool," said Martin, not knowing how else to respond.

"Yeah, but it's getting lame over here. I'm going to go to my grandmom's cottage. You two can come along if you feel like it."

Martin and Randy eyed each other. Randy bugged his eyes out, and Martin wiggled his nose and tutted.

"Yeah, why not. We don't have anything else to do," Martin said.

"She's usually got Beaver Pops in the freezer," she said, hopping off the picnic table bench and starting off toward a small thicket.

III. The Dangerous Person

Zargothni and the boys strode across the field that led to the cottage, but all the while evil eyes were upon them. They were being watched closely, and heavy breathing could be heard as a voiceover if you were lucky enough to be in the audience and not be one of those stalked by this dangerous person. You could tell the dangerous person was wearing a mask because the field of vision was limited to two eyeholes, which tracked the party from a safe or, rather, a *dangerous* distance. The three youths appeared oblivious, laughing about rock music or something youthful like that.

"Well, this is it," Zargothni told the boys when they reached a hovel dug into a butte. Earthen walls, live grass roof.

"Your family are hobbits?" asked Martin.

"She's just old-fashioned. Also, I should warn you—she's a Christmas bride."

"What's that mean?" Randy asked.

Martin shrugged.

Zargothni opened the door and said in a singsong voice, "We're here!"

It was much homier on the inside than the boys would have suspected. Despite roots growing from the ceiling, into which were tied hams and dried fruits, the hut was furnished comfortably and decorated with a crafty, grandmotherly touch.

"I smell gingerbread," muttered Martin.

"Is this lady a witch?" murmured Randy.

A small, fancy Cherrywood door swung open to reveal the grandmother. She was very short, white-haired, and wore a filthy wedding dress with dried up holly and pinecones festooning the disintegrating veil.

"Hello, my darling! Come give Grandmom a hug!"

Zargothni squeezed the old woman, lifting her off the ground.

"My, my!" Grandmom said. "You are getting so big! Soon, you can carry me all around the house. My corns are getting quite bad, you know."

Zargothni set the woman down and introduced the two boys, but she got their names mixed up, so it took a few minutes of explanation before everyone was sure they knew who they were again.

"I've made a spice cake!" Grandmom announced. "Isn't it perfectly exciting that you showed up when I was making a spice cake?"

"Yes. Thanks, ma'am," Randy said. "We are very hungry."

"You are all welcome to have some, of course, but we'll have to wait until Christmas gets here."

"That's months and months away," Martin said.

Zargothni cleared her throat. "I told them you were a Christmas bride, but I don't think they understood."

"You see, boys, I'm a Christmas bride. Have you ever heard a sailor say he was married to the sea? That's me and Christmas. Christmas is my husband. So once he gets home, we can eat cake, but not before. It would be disrespectful."

Martin eyed the old woman warily. He noticed a glassy deadness to her eyes, the kind he'd always associated with sharks.

Zargothni leaned in close and whispered to them, "Just humor her."

"Oh. Uh, congratulations!" Randy said.

"And of course," Grandmom said excitedly, "I have presents for all of you! Let me snatch them from the bedroom!" She whisked herself away with surprising speed for such a tiny, ancient woman.

"Okay," Zargothni said gruffly. "Here's the deal. She was supposed to get married to a rich old guy on Christmas, but he never showed up. She was jilted and has never taken that dress off since. She never married, and she went a little nuts, living as an old spinster."

"Wait, what about your granddad?" Martin asked.

"What about him?"

"She's your grandmother, right? So, at some point, she had to sleep with a guy and give birth to one of your parents. That's how grandparenthood works."

"Ah," she said, stumped. "Good point. I have no idea how she's my grandmother. But she is, I'm pretty sure."

"What became of the rich guy who was supposed to marry her?" Randy said.

"He was trampled by reindeer."

"Man, that's messed up."

"I'm back!" Grandmom called to them. "Here are your gifts!" She handed them each a box about the size of a softball. Zargothni's was wrapped in shiny purple paper with a lavender ribbon. Randy's was wrapped in blue paper with white bells on it. Martin's was wrapped in green and gold paper covered in a geometric pattern that most people hadn't seen since about 1985.

"Go ahead," Grandmom urged. "Open them."

Randy was the first to get his open.

"Oh. A softball."

Martin was next.

"Yea! Another softball."

Zargothni opened hers and said, "We can play a game of softball vs. softball. We each throw our balls at one another's faces and hope that we can smack them together midair and not get our teeth busted out."

"That was your favorite game when you were a little girl," Grandmom said. "Don't think I've forgotten."

"Well, I'm not a little girl anymore. I'm practically a woman. I'm right on the verge of womanhood. I wish there were a word for it."

"Hobblehoyden?" Martin proposed.

"Meh, I guess that works."

The door opened, and an anthropomorphic conifer tree entered the room, removing a large red sack from its shoulder and setting it on the floor.

"Um, Christmas?" said Zargothni.

"Why yes," said the tree. "Pleased to meet you, young miss."

"Oh, Christmas, my dear!" Grandmom said. "I'm so glad you are home. And you've chosen such a joyous form to take this time!" She rushed to give him a great big hug and made a horrible noise as branches poked her nose and mouth.

"Sorry, wife! That's the problem with taking the form of a living tree."

"Think nothing of it. I'm just so glad you are home. Now we can have cake."

The cake was fucking delicious. Then Grandmom brought out Beaver Pops for the kids, and suddenly it seemed to them that this was the best Christmas ever. Christmas himself was having a jolly good time, even if he was behaving suspiciously.

"I have something important to tell you all!" Christmas said suddenly, rising from his seat at the dessert table and grabbing the knife that had been used to cut the cake.

"What on earth, honey?" Grandmom chirped.

"I—"

A loud knock at the door interrupted.

"Well, who could that be in the middle of Christmas dessert?" Grandmom said, quite annoyed. She toddled over to the door and revealed the author of the story.

"I'm sorry to interrupt," he said bashfully. "This all is going so splendidly, but you see, we are at the end of quite a long collection at this point, and I'd originally intended this piece to be closer to three thousand words. We are going to have to end it here."

"What?" said the boys. "We need to know what happens to us next!"

"Um," said the author, "the Christmas guy, he's trying to kill you all. It's Michale Horns in disguise—that guy from the first part who was doing the magic show. He's out to kill you both for some reason."

"Why?" Martin asked.

"Not really clear. Anyway, it doesn't matter at this point. Because now, you all live happily ever after."

"Do I get the girl?" Randy asked.

The author's eyes widened.

"Oh, sure," he replied. "And women don't vote or drive cars anymore. What are you, some kind of reactionary?"

"I'm just a kid! I didn't ask to be written!" he ran from the room, screaming as the scene faded from existence, never to be remembered again unless someone decides to reread this for some reason.

Oh well.

END

AFTERWORD

I'd like to thank all my fans, compatriots,
and supporters who stuck by me over the years. Here it is, my sixth book. I
couldn't do it without you.

Specific thanks to Vince, the Charleses, Kara,
Jason, Sophia, Dustin, Brad, and Doug.

I wouldn't be writing what I write without
a few touchstones from my tender years: Lewis Carroll, The
Twilight Zone, Monty Python's Flying Circus, The Far Side, Hitchhiker's Guide
to the Galaxy, and Ren & Stimpy. As I got older: the writing of Franz
Kafka, Jorge Luis Borges, Donald Barthelme, Kelly Link, Brian Evenson, and Ray
Fracalossy; the films of Guy Maddin, David Lynch, Quentin Dupieux, David
Cronenberg, Terry Gilliam, and Takashi Miike; the television of PFFR (from whom
I yoinked the title of this collection), Tim & Eric, and AdultSwim in
general; the music of The Jesus Lizard, The Residents, Ween, and Mr. Bungle.

Here's hoping that bizarre writing and
films continue to become more and more common in this decade as they have for
the previous two. Forget the haters, the social climbers, the scolds, the
conspiracists, and the attention-seekers. Just make weird art, for the sake of
Cripes!
Miss you, Mom.

ABOUT THE AUTHOR

G. Arthur Brown writes absurd, surreal fiction from the comfort of the edge of sanity in the Pacific Northwest under the influence of Kafka, Barthelme, Lynch, and Link. When he's not writing, he's plugging his guitar into effects pedals or chopping vegetables. This is his sixth book and second collection.

PUBLISHING CREDITS

1. The Haunted Monster (<u>Mondo Bizarro</u>, ed. M. P. Johnson, Rooster Republic)
2. I Took One Apple to the Grave (<u>Four Gentlemen of the Apocalypse</u>, Strange Edge)
3. I Took A CHEMTRAIL and Now I Dead (<u>I Took A CHEMTRAIL and Now I Dead</u> chapbook, Strange Edge)
4. Bronson's Shark Tank (<u>Surreal Grotesque Magazine</u>)
5. Governor of the Homeless (<u>Governor of the Homeless</u> limited release illustrated chapbook, Psychedelic Horror Press)
6. Chemtrail Chameleon (<u>Chemtrail Chameleon</u> chapbook, Strange Edge)
7. The Story of Job (previously unpublished)
8. The Pitfalls of Modern Gardening (<u>Bizarro Bizarro</u>, ed. Rocky Alexander, Bizarro Pulp Press)
9. Harbinger Master (<u>Axes of Evil</u>, ed. Alex S. Johnson, Diabolus in Musica)
10. Dead Bug Detective (previously unpublished, early version debuted orally at The Ultimate Bizarro Showdown at BizarroCon)

NEW AND COMING SOON FROM PLANET BIZARRO

CPSIA information can be obtained
at www.ICGtesting.com
Printed in the USA
LVHW100602240522
719535LV00005B/119